## *"You must be the Bear."*

Jim Standing Bear knew Sarah Sloan had not come to his house to give him hope; she'd come to offer him pity. Jim's scowl deepened. What had he been thinking of, leaving his hiding place, exposing himself to the raw emotions of a woman?

"Yes," he finally replied.

"I'm your new neighbor," Sarah said. "I apologize for coming over uninvited, but you haven't been coming to your rooftop, and I was worried that something might have happened."

Sarah looked straight into his eyes. He searched her face and saw not one shred of pity.

Still, Jim couldn't unbend. *Wouldn't* unbend. Embattled warriors never gave an inch. That's how he saw himself now. Though at the moment he couldn't have said whether his battle was with his wheelchair or the merciless attraction that was turning his blood to fire.

Retreat was out of the question. Attack was his only option.

"As you can see, something *did* happen."

Dear Reader,

While every romance holds the promise of sweeping readers away with a rugged alpha male or a charismatic cowboy, this month we want to take a closer look at the women who fall in love with our favorite heroes.

"Heroines need to be strong," says Sherryl Woods, author of more than fifty novels. "Readers look for a woman who can stand up to the hero—and stand up to life." Sherryl's book *A Love Beyond Words* features a special heroine who lost her hearing but became stronger because of it. "A heroine needs to triumph over fear or adversity."

Kate Stockwell faces the fear of knowing she cannot bear her own child in Allison Leigh's *Her Unforgettable Fiancé,* the next installment in the STOCKWELLS OF TEXAS miniseries. And an accident forces Josie Scott, Susan Mallery's LONE STAR CANYON heroine in *Wife in Disguise,* to take stock of her life and find a second chance....

In Peggy Webb's *Standing Bear's Surrender,* Sarah Sloan must choose between loyalty and true love! In *Separate Bedrooms...?* by Carole Halston, Cara LaCroix is faced with fulfilling her grandmother's final wish—marriage! And Kirsten Laurence needs the help of the man who broke her heart years ago in Laurie Campbell's *Home at Last.*

"A heroine is a real role model," Sherryl says. And in Special Edition, we aim for every heroine to be a woman we can all admire. Here's to strong women and many more emotionally satisfying reads from Silhouette Special Edition!

Karen Taylor Richman
Senior Editor

Please address questions and book requests to:
Silhouette Reader Service
U.S.: 3010 Walden Ave., P.O. Box 1325, Buffalo, NY 14269
Canadian: P.O. Box 609, Fort Erie, Ont. L2A 5X3

# Standing Bear's Surrender

## PEGGY WEBB

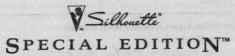

*Silhouette*

# SPECIAL EDITION™

Published by Silhouette Books

America's Publisher of Contemporary Romance

This book is dedicated to my editors at Silhouette, who encourage, applaud, sympathize, run interference and in general make me a better writer. Tara, Karen and Janet, this one's for you.

Acknowledgments: To Olivia and Alex for pulling the cow out of the ditch. To Ruth Ann for putting salve on her wounds. And to my children and grandchildren for loving support. Always.

 SILHOUETTE BOOKS

ISBN 0-373-24384-7

STANDING BEAR'S SURRENDER

**Books by Peggy Webb**

## PEGGY WEBB

and her two chocolate Labs live in a hundred-year-old house not far from the farm where she grew up. "A farm is a wonderful place for dreaming," she says. "I used to sit in the hayloft and dream of being a writer." Now, with two grown children and more than forty-five romance novels to her credit, the former English teacher confesses she's still a hopeless romantic and loves to create the happy endings her readers love so well.

When she isn't writing, she can be found at her piano playing blues and jazz or in one of her gardens planting flowers. A believer in the idea that a person should never stand still, Peggy recently taught herself carpentry.

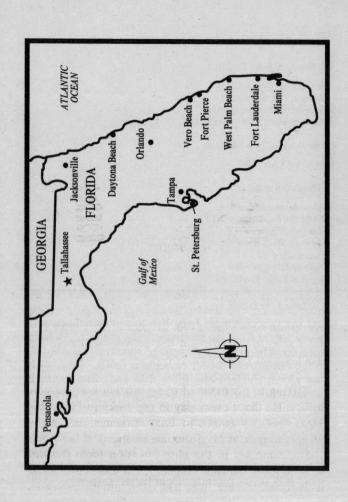

## Prologue

The storm blew up suddenly out of the Gulf, whipping sheets of rain across I10, rain so hard and so thick Jim could barely see a foot in front of his headlights. He tightened his grip on the steering wheel of his black Jaguar convertible.

"Don't let me down now, baby."

Talking to his mode of transportation was not new to Jim. He did it every day in the cockpit of the F/A-18 Hornet, sometimes in English, sometimes in the ancient tongue of his Sioux ancestors.

His comrades in the elite precision flight demonstration team, the Blue Angels, often teased him about it. Especially Chuck, who had given him the nickname that stuck—the Bear, short for Jim Standing Bear.

"Hey, Bear," he'd say. "Put a little of that Sioux voodoo on my plane. I think I'm gonna need it today."

There was an easy camaraderie among Blue Angels,

for all of them had one thing in common—they lived to fly. There was also a strong bond of trust. The maneuvers they did in the Hornets were extremely dangerous. There was no room for mistakes. Miscalculation meant death.

That's why he and Chuck and the rest of the gang were extremely careful. Always.

Until tonight.

Tonight Jim Standing Bear didn't have the luxury of caution. If he didn't show up at his engagement party in Mobile, Bethany Lawrence would kill him. It was that simple.

He sensed the eighteen-wheeler before he saw its headlights. It was a monstrous shape in the rain, bearing down on him too fast.

"Slow down, fool." The words were barely out of Jim's mouth when the driver of the rig pulled into the passing lane, his trailer rocking with too much speed and not enough traction.

Jim saw what was going to happen to him. In the split second before the rig smashed into his Jag, he saw his situation: a small car with the Bay on one side and the rig on the other. He was trapped.

The impact flung his car against the railing. Metal ground against metal. Jim's last conscious thought was a prayer that the railing would hold.

Then his car broke apart, and Jim Standing Bear with it.

Pain so intense he could hardly bear it. Blinding lights. Footsteps day and night. Rubber soles squeaking against tile. Tubes and needles. Brain fogged. Drifting. For days on end. Drifting.

"Welcome back to the world."

His brother Ben was standing over him, looking haggard and too thin.

"What happened to you?" Jim said. "You look like hell."

"Listen to the man. Hooked up to IVs and worried about his baby brother." Ben clasped Jim's hand.

"That hurts like hell. Every damned inch of me hurts."

The fog that had obscured his brain for days had finally lifted, and it all came back: the rainy night, the drunk driver, the crash.

"I made it." It was a simple statement that showed nothing of Jim's feelings, nothing of the wonder...and the dread.

Men didn't walk away from crashes of that nature unscathed.

"Yes, pal, you made it."

Jim could read his baby brother like a book. "Spit it out. What's my condition?"

"You're doing great for somebody whose car looks like a squashed tuna can."

"If you can't do better than that, you're going to make one hell of a lousy doctor."

"Your left side took the biggest beating."

Jim listened while Ben described in detail the broken bones, the fractures and contusions, the concussion, the ruptured spleen. He listened while his brother told of the procedures to repair the damage.

But mostly he watched his brother's face. And a cold fear unlike any he'd ever known gripped Jim.

"My legs. You didn't mention my legs."

"The doctors say the surgery was very successful."

"Be specific. And don't soft-peddal."

His brother described the exact placement of pins and the physical therapy he would need.

"You'll be walking again before you know it."

Jim closed his eyes to hide his private hell. He would never fly his F/A-18 Hornet again. The G forces were so great that grown men in less than top-notch physical condition had been known to pass out.

Life as he knew it was over.

"Where's Bethany? I want to see Bethany."

"She's not here right now, Jim."

"Call her. Tell her I want to see her."

"I can't. She's in New York. With her folks."

"In New York?"

"Yeah, pal. I guess the pressure got to her. She'll be back. I'm sure of it."

Jim was too tired to wonder at Ben's last statement. A nurse came into the room with another round of painkillers, and Jim closed his eyes and drifted into blessed oblivion.

The first person he saw when the fog lifted again was his fiancée, looking even more beautiful than he remembered.

"Hello, gorgeous." Jim said.

"Jim." She stood two feet away, twisting her engagement ring on her finger. "How do you feel?"

"Like I've been run through a sausage grinder. How are you holding up, darling?"

Bethany winced. "Jim, don't."

"Don't what?"

"Say those things. I can't...I can't..." She covered her face with her hands and began to sob.

Jim wanted to comfort her, but she was still out of his reach. All he could do was hold out his hand.

"Come here, kiddo."

"I can't Jim. I can't do this." She twisted the ring off her finger and laid it in his outstretched hand. "I can't be married to a cripple."

She flew out of the room as if demons chased her. And Jim supposed they did. The demons of uncertainty and inconvenience. If there was anything Bethany Lawrence hated it was inconvenience.

After the door shut behind her, Jim remembered that the tears hadn't even streaked her makeup. Bethany always did believe in waterproof mascara.

The ring, a two-carat emerald-cut diamond, was a painful reminder of everything Jim had lost—his fiancée, his career, his future. Jim clenched his hand into a fist to hide the ring, then closed his eyes and prayed for the blessed oblivion of sleep.

# Chapter One

Ben set the new telescope firmly in place on the roof-top garden of Jim's house that overlooked Pensacola Bay, then defied Jim to protest with one of his *I'm-talking-scalps* looks.

"What am I supposed to do with that damned thing?" Jim asked.

"Study the stars." Ben focused the telescope and took a peek at the sky. "Get your butt over here and take a look before I come over there and drag you over."

"You and what navy?"

Their sparring was good-natured and natural. Humor was a coping mechanism they'd learned growing up in the orphanage.

Jim maneuvered his wheelchair to the telescope and focused on the sky, even though rain clouds obscured all but a few stars. He could feel Ben watching him.

He shoved the telescope aside and turned to his brother.

"Go ahead. Say it."

"All right, I will. It's been six months. Why don't you get out of that chair and walk?"

"I'll give you one word: *crackup.*"

"The orthopedic surgeon tells me there's no physical reason you can't walk, Jim."

"Are you saying I'm a damned emotional cripple?" Jim said, then quick remorse slashed him. He softened his tone.

"Go on, Ben, get out of here. Go to the movies, have a drink down at Trader Bill's, pick up a girl."

Jim turned back to the telescope. "I'll be good. See. I promise to sit up here and look through this thing for two hours if you'll just get out of the house. Is it a deal?"

"Deal. And don't you cheat. I'll expect a full report when I get back." Ben left, whistling.

Jim wouldn't think of cheating. He owed his brother. Ben had stayed out of medical school the fall semester after Jim's accident, and would have stayed out the spring semester, as well, if Jim hadn't made him go back.

He swiveled the telescope idly, adjusted focus, not seeing anything except darkening clouds. Then he saw it, a tiny pinpoint of light. He would report the star in complete detail to Ben. Suddenly his mouth went dry and sweat beaded his face. The pinpoint of light was not a star: it was the lights on a Skyhawk, going into Pensacola Air Base for a landing.

Jim shoved the telescope away with clenched fists. The feeling of loss made him weak, and he gripped the arms of his chair, remembering.

*"You don't need the chair, Jim,"* his doctor had said.

*"Then why am I in it? Why won't my legs move?"*

*"An educated guess. You can't fly so you can't walk."*

The roar of jets came to him, the heart-in-throat moment of lifting toward the sky, and suddenly... He owned the universe. That's how it had been. That's how it would never be again.

Blindly he looked next door, down into a brick-enclosed garden. Anywhere except up.

Gradually he became aware of the ancient walls, the tangled growth and the empty fountain presided over by an angel with a broken wing. All of it was illuminated by floodlights.

The house had been empty for months. New neighbors must have moved in. Of course, the brick wall hid the garden from view except from his rooftop. And this was the first time he'd been up here since his accident. Six months, to be exact.

Idly he trained his telescope into the garden, focusing on the angel. She was life-sized, perfectly proportioned, her bare feet and stone legs covered with lichen. The broken wing gave her a rakish quality, as if she might know things other angels didn't know, as if she had rather be off playing pranks instead of flying around guarding mere mortals.

Jim rubbed his hands over his face. Fatigue always caught him unaware. He used to take his body for granted. He ran six miles a day without thinking, did a hundred pushups without breaking a sweat, swam without thought of the powerful legs that propelled him through the water. He'd always been an athlete.

Until the accident took that away, along with his career, his fiancée, and everything else that mattered.

Everything except his brother.

Jim put his eye to the lens of the telescope. The angel's face looked different. Softer. Gentler. He rubbed his eyes once more. Maybe his vision was blurring. Since the accident, sometimes it did.

He looked through the scope once more, and that's when he saw the angel move.

This was no angel. This was a flesh-and-blood woman. And not merely moving. She was dancing.

Feeling guilty as if he'd been caught spying, Jim shoved back from the telescope.

He could still see the woman in the garden. She wore something white and soft looking, a summer dress or perhaps a gown. And even though it was early March and the rain clouds threatened, her arms were bare. She was going to get wet. Not that it mattered. Certainly not to Jim.

Who was the man she was dancing with? A husband? A father? A brother? Why had he let her come out into the rainy night without a wrap? The clouds that had been gathering all evening released their burden, and rain began to fall softly on the earth.

The woman turned her face upward to the rain, and against his will Jim found himself focusing on her through his telescope. Every line in her body conveyed a vibrancy that mesmerized. And she was laughing.

Over the past few months he'd almost forgotten how to laugh. Instead he'd learned despair in all its guises.

Her laughter drifted over the garden wall like bells, like music, and something in him yearned toward the distant sound.

Round and round she twirled as if she were dancing in the ballroom of a fancy hotel instead of across the broken brick pathways of a tangled garden. It was the waltz. Jim used to dance it often. Back when he could.

Mesmerized, Jim focused the telescope on her once more. He couldn't help himself. Blame it on the night. Blame it on the rain. Blame it on a miracle: the first faint stirrings of interest he'd had since his accident.

The woman's hair was dark brown, straight and as sleek as the pelt of an otter. Her arms were slender and pale. Obviously she was not the kind of woman who worshipped the sun. Probably the only time she bared her arms was in the cool of the evening, long after the burning sun had vanished.

What in the world was she doing in Florida? Why was she dancing alone in an overgrown garden? And who was the man at her side?

Jim started to focus on the man, then shoved the telescope away. What was the matter with him? He was no damned voyeur.

Still, something kept drawing him back to the woman. Curiosity? His own loneliness manifesting itself in a morbid fashion? He didn't know. All he knew was that he couldn't leave the rooftop as long as the woman was in the garden, dancing in the rain.

With his hands gripping the arms of his wheelchair and his own head bared to the rain, Jim Standing Bear sat on his rooftop and watched the distant figure in white twirling around her garden.

Occasionally the wind caught the sound of her laughter and wafted it to Jim's rooftop perch. It was balm to his battered soul.

* * *

Sarah held her father tightly, careful of the bricks. That's the last thing she needed: broken bones.

"You dance very well, Ginger," he said.

"So do you, Fred."

Her father laughed. "Why shouldn't I? I'm the best of them all. I'm the man who danced on the ceiling."

Sarah's heart broke a little. The man who thought he was Fred Astair was Dr. Eric Sloan, one of the greatest heart surgeons in America. And one of the finest men in the world.

He was more than a father to her. He was her friend, mentor, co-worker. He was her entire world.

Except for her sister Julie, of course.

The confrontation she'd had with her sister earlier in the day played through her mind.

"You shouldn't encourage him in his fantasies," Julie had said.

"If I try to correct him, he gets upset. The truth only confuses and saddens him, Julie."

"How is he ever going to keep things straight if you play these little games with him, Sarah?"

"That's just it, Julie. Dad is never going to keep things straight. Never."

Julie began to cry, and even crying she looked like one of the glamorous stars who had stepped down from the screen of the movie, *The Great Gatsby*.

Sarah put her arms around her sister. Giving comfort. Receiving comfort. They both cried awhile, then Sarah was the first to recover.

"We'll get through this together, Julie. Three against the world. Remember?"

That brought a smile to Julie's face.

"Yeah, three Musketeers, three little pigs, three little bears."

Now they were both smiling. Julie had been seven and Sarah a newborn when Helen Sloan died. Eric had stepped into the gap, moving his office back home to be with his girls.

"Three against the world," he'd say to them, and they'd all join hands and dance around the living room.

Eric Sloan had not only been a superb doctor but a superb dancer as well. Now it was the only memory he had. Dancing. Sarah wasn't about to take that away from him.

She'd glanced at her father, leaning against the grand piano in Julie's house, his feet tapping to the rhythmn of imaginary music. Seeing the direction of her gaze, Julie sobered.

"I just don't know what to do. Tell me, Sarah. You've always known how to cope."

Her sister had summarized Sarah's life in one sentence. Give Sarah a problem and she could solve it. Put her in the midst of chaos and she could organize it. Present her with an emergency and she could survive it.

What she couldn't do was bat her eyes and have the world swoon at her feet. She couldn't turn heads and set hearts a-flutter. She couldn't win parts in plays and be the life of the party. She couldn't even follow her dream.

As long as she could remember she'd wanted to be a professional dancer, not necessarily a prima ballerina, but one of the line, dancing onstage with spotlights glittering like stars, shining straight to her heart.

After years of study and hard work, she'd gone to her first audition in New York. Waiting backstage hidden behind the curtain she'd overheard the other girls talking. "What does Sarah Sloan think this is? The barnyard ballet? She'll never make the cut. She's too homely."

She *hadn't* made it. Not that day nor all the days and weeks afterward. She'd left New York, gone back to school and become the best teacher anybody could want.

But the words had sunk into her soul. No matter where she was, what she did, Sarah remembered.

Her father's voice brought her back to the garden where the two of them danced his fantasy.

"It's raining, Ginger," her father said.

"Yes, it is. We'd better go back inside before you catch a chill."

"Can I stay a while longer?" Her father sat on the bench beneath the stone angel. "I want to watch you dance."

Her father had always loved to watch her dance. It was another memory he hadn't lost. Sarah opened the umbrella for her father, then turned back to the garden and began to dance just as she did in her dreams, her movements free and easy, her face shining with tears.

She couldn't have said whether she was crying in sad exultation that her father remembered how she had once danced, or whether she was crying for the girl she had once been.

The rain came down harder.

"It's time to go inside, Dad."

Instead of feeling chilled she suddenly felt energized. She was in a new home, a new place. Pensacola had good medical facilities, good doctors.

She would hire someone to help with her dad, then

she would find a job. Good teachers were always in demand.

Meanwhile she had this private haven, a lovely secret garden. She would transform it into a wonderland. A stage. A place of dreams.

"You're still up here?" Ben hurried onto the rooftop patio. "Man, you don't even have a jacket. You're going to catch cold."

He pulled off his jacket and tossed it to Jim. "Let's get off this roof. I've got microwave popcorn and a Roy Rogers video waiting downstairs."

"What more could a man want?"

Ben punched the button, and they got onto the elevator. "You sound almost cheerful. The telescope did some good, huh?"

Jim thought of the woman. She'd stayed in the garden almost two hours, dancing. Even after she went inside, Jim hadn't wanted to leave the spot where he'd watched her in secret.

"You might say that."

On the bottom floor, the brothers went into the kitchen where they dried off with towels Ben retrieved from the adjoining laundry room. Afterward he turned his attention to popping corn.

"You'll never guess who's living next door," he said.

"Are you going to make me?"

*"Dr. Eric Sloan.* My God, the man's a legend, and he's living right next door to you."

Relief washed over Jim. The woman's partner had been her father.

He didn't have to be in the medical profession to know of the famous doctor. He'd pioneered a technique in the field of cardiology that had given him worldwide acclaim.

"I thought he was doing mission work somewhere in Mexico."

"La Joya. He's been down there for years with one of his daughters, but he developed Alzheimer's and she brought him back to the States."

Jim wondered if that was the daughter he'd seen in the garden. What did it matter? Disgusted at himself, he wheeled into the den.

Ben called after him. "The popcorn's not finished. Don't start without me."

"I wouldn't think of it, kid. Don't I always take care of you?"

Jim had been taking care of his younger brother since their parents had died when a roller-coaster left its tracks at the state fair. Two-year-old Ben hadn't let go of his twelve-year-old brother's hand until six months after they'd settled into the orphanage.

The smell of popcorn preceded Ben into the room. "I put extra butter on yours, Jim." He handed his brother a bowl, then settled into an easy chair with his feet up. "By the way, I saw Chuck at Trader Bill's tonight. He asked about you.

Commander Chuck Sayers, lead solo pilot in the Number Five plane and was one of Jim's closest friends.

"They're all asking about you, Jim. They're wondering why you won't see them."

*Because they remind me of everything I've lost,* Jim thought, *of conquering the skies, of flying into sunsets and sunrises and heavens so achingly beautiful they make a grown man cry, of touching the face of God.*

"What did you tell them?"

"I told them you were working so hard at your physical therapy you hardly had time for anything else, that you barely had time for me."

"Thanks, kid."

Ben put the movie in, then settled back into his chair with the remote control. "Don't thank me, Jim. I'm not going to keep making excuses for you. You're getting out of this house if I have to kick your butt." Ben threw a handful of popcorn at him.

Jim lobbed a few grains at his brother. "You and which navy?"

Ben began to rattle off the names of the Blue Angels. "Chuck, Glenn, Russell..."

"Start the movie. It's late and I'm tired and we'll have to clean up all this popcorn before Delta comes."

Delta, the maid. The only woman Jim knew who could put the fear of God into him.

"What's all that popcorn doing in the den?" Delta marched into the weight room without knocking and stood in front of the machine Jim was working on with her arms crossed and her lips poked out a mile. In love with pattern and color, she wore a red polka-dotted scarf over her gray fuzzy hair and a neon yellow apron over green- and purple-striped slacks. "You got butter all over that divan and I don't know how I'm gonna clean it up short of burning it."

"Burn it," Jim said. "I don't care."

"You don't care about nothing since you lost your legs."

Delta didn't pussyfoot around. She was the only person who referred to Jim's condition as if it were natural. He appreciated her candor. More than that, he appreciated her loyalty. She'd been taking care of him and his house for more than fifteen years without ever missing a cleaning day.

"Don't expect a Christmas bonus from me this year, Delta."

"Humph, I ain't expecting nothing from you but a lot of lip." Delta lingered under the pretext of dusting the barbells. It was her way of checking on Jim, and about as subtle as an elephant in the living room. "You better be worried about me quitting. I got another job, and I hear tell they're nice people with manners, unlike some folks I know."

If anybody else had suggested leaving Jim, Delta would have had their head on a platter.

"Anybody I know, Delta?"

"If you don't, you ought to. They're just on the other side of that brick wall."

The weights clanked together as Jim missed a beat. He was going to be sharing a maid with the woman next door. In addition to being the best housekeeper in Pensacola, Delta was also the nosiest. And the most talkative. He could find out everything he wanted to know about the woman in the garden. Including her name.

That is, if he wanted to know.

Did he? The answer was no. He had absolutely no interest in her except as a fascinating subject to view from afar.

That particular subject occupied his mind for the better part of the day, and as soon as dark came, he was in his rooftop garden with the telescope.

The garden next door was empty. Jim started to wheel back inside, but suddenly there she was standing among the ruins that had once been a beautiful garden.

The woman next door. Dancing. And this time she was alone.

She was lithe and graceful, and she danced with such passion that Jim was moved to tears.

He lost track of time. There was only the night, the woman and the moon turning her silver.

He stayed until long after she went inside, and when he went to bed all his dreams were filled with her.

Sarah was apprehensive about meeting the house-keeper. "You're going to like Delta," Julie had said. "Unlike most housekeepers, she'll do anything you ask her. She'll be a big help with Dad."

The doorbell rang, and there on her doorstep stood the most outrageous woman Sarah had ever seen. She was wearing so many colors she looked like a rainbow.

"Hi, I'm Delta and this is your lucky day. Miss Julie tells me you got a poor old sick daddy that don't hardly even know he's in the world, and I'm here to tell you that folks like that don't scare me none. I love everybody, and God's pitiful creatures most of all."

Delta strode into the hall, hung her purple hat on the hat rack, then surveyed her surroundings, shaking her head. "Lord, honey, you sure can use some help."

"We've just moved in. I haven't unpacked all the boxes, and I'm afraid I got sidetracked in the garden."

"Delta's here now. You don't have to worry about a thing, Miss Sarah."

"Call me Sarah." Sometimes when the heart is overburdened, a small kindness can reduce a person to tears. That's how Sarah felt now, but she blinked the tears back. "You don't know what a relief it is to have you here, Delta."

"I wish that stubborn man next door could hear this. He don't listen to a thing I say. If he don't start trying to live again, I don't know what's going to become of him."

Sarah had visions of a gray-haired man, much like her father, who had suffered an illness that took his body but not his mind. She had always been a romantic. She could take the least little bit of information and build an entire fantasy around it. And while she abhorred gossip she *was* interested in her neighbors, especially the ones on either side of her new house.

Not that she would pump the housekeeper for information. Fortunately, Delta didn't need pumping.

"You might have heard of him, your sister living here and all."

Sarah shook her head. "I've been living out of the country for years."

"Jim Standing Bear, the Bear, they call him. He's one of the Blue Angels. Now, I *know* you've heard of them." Sarah nodded. "He was one of the sweetest men I ever knew till that wreck tore him all to pieces. Now, I ain't one to gossip, but I worry about my babies, and he's one of my babies. Mm-hmm. Been taking care of him for might 'nigh onto sixteen years, and I ain't never seen a handsomer, kinder man. Jim Standing Bear is a gentleman through and through and anybody tells me different is gonna get walloped upside the head. It like to killed me and him both when he had to quit flying."

Sarah'd heart contracted. She had always been partial to angels with broken wings.

"Will he ever fly again?"

"I don't know if he's gonna *walk* again, let alone fly."

"Oh, dear." Now, Sarah did get tears in her eyes. It was always easier to cry for somebody else. She revised her vision of the gray-haired man to somebody much younger, a tall muscular man with black hair and the blackest eyes she'd ever seen, the kind of man she used to secretly drool over at the Saturday matinee. She pictured him in Navy dress blues with gold wings pinned to his shoulder.

Upstairs, a bell began to ring. "That's Dad. I have to go."

"You go on up, honey, and don't worry about a thing. I'll start in the kitchen."

Upstairs she found her father sitting in a chair beside the window. He smiled when she came in, not the vacant smile she'd seen for the last few weeks, but the real smile full of wit and understanding.

"I'm sorry to ring, Sarah, darling, but these old legs are not what they used to be."

She knelt beside his chair and kissed his gnarled hands. "Dad, it's wonderful to have you back."

"I'm afraid these moments of lucidity will become more and more infrequent. I wonder if you can accompany me into the garden and read to me? I want to take advantage of every moment I have left."

"You know I will." Sarah lifted a copy of Homer's *The Odyssey* with a well-worn leather cover, then led her father down the curving marble staircase.

The sun was brilliant, the day was warm, especially for March, and even in its unkempt state, the garden was beautiful. She guided her father to the fountain, then sat beneath the angel with the broken wing and began to read.

Her father tilted his face up to the sun and closed his eyes, smiling. Sarah's heart lifted. Coming to Florida had been the right thing to do. Her father loved the outdoors, and the sun had a therapeutic effect on people. Who knew what miracles might occur?

In the midst of the chapter about Circe's enchantment, Sarah felt another presence. It was more than a prickle at the back of her neck, more than the shiver that ran down her spine, more than the goose bumps that popped up on her arms. Awareness invaded her, filled her soul, took over her skin, a bone-deep certainty that she was no longer alone. Her father had long since fallen asleep, and she'd continued reading merely for the sound of a human voice, even if it was her own.

Sarah kept her eyes on the book, but she was no longer reading. Nor was she capable, for the powerful presence stole her breath. A potbellied stove had taken up residence where her heart used to be, and heat radiated through every pore of her body.

She'd meant to keep her head down. She'd meant to keep reading, but something beyond her control made Sarah glance upward, and there he was sitting on his rooftop. Her next-door neighbor. Standing Bear, the Blue Angel.

It wasn't polite to stare. That's what she'd been taught, but Sarah couldn't have turned away if she were being chased by a stampede of wild elephants. He was no more than a distant figure, but Sarah didn't need to see every detail to know him. She knew him already, deep in her bones. There was great strength in the man and even greater courage. But most of all there was great kindness.

It was no accident that the Bear had for a time been

one of the elite flying Blue Angels, for that's exactly what he was—an angel. Sarah's own personal guardian angel.

She realized that the Bear had probably come to his rooftop to take advantage of the sun. She knew he was a mortal man with a broken body. She knew he was probably doing well to take care of himself, let alone somebody else.

Still, she could dream, couldn't she? Life was too hard not to take advantage of every glimmer of the rainbow. First the garden and then the guardian angel, the real thing, not a cold stone statue.

With the Bear's warmth still on her skin, Sarah closed the book and stood up. She would attack the weeds. She would wrestle with the overgrown vines. She would unearth the rose beds and give the camellias room to breathe.

But first she would acknowledge her angel. Looking across the garden wall and upward toward the Bear, she smiled.

## Chapter Two

Thirty minutes earlier when he'd shoved aside his monthly bills and headed to the rooftop, Jim had told himself that if the woman was in the garden next door, he would leave. He was not a voyeur.

She was there reading to an elderly man who was probably her father. And Jim couldn't make himself leave. Wearing a pink dress with a matching pink sweater covering her arms, just as he'd suspected, she looked like a rose blooming among the ruins, a bright spot of hope in the midst of desolation.

And so he'd stayed, watching her in secret, telling himself that if she looked up and noticed him, *then* he would leave. Her hair slid forward as she bent over her book, revealing a neck as graceful as a swan's. Jim couldn't resist a closer look. The view through the telescope confirmed his earlier opinion. The back of

her neck was fair and soft looking. Jim's heart
pounded harder and his mouth went dry.

Disgusted with himself he shoved back from the
telescope, but he didn't leave. He couldn't. The sun
was shining in the woman's hair and he'd never seen
a more mesmerizing sight. The hair that had looked
merely dark at night came alive in the glare of the sun.
Strands of red glinted there, and gold in every shade
from the deep glow of a full harvest moon to the rich
patina of an ancient wedding band.

Need sliced him. The need to touch her hair.

Jim gripped the arms of his wheelchair so hard his
knuckles turned white. He would turn away. He *had*
to.

And then she smiled. Straight at him. There was no
mistaking it. The woman in the garden deliberately
looked his way and smiled.

All the breath left Jim's body. Suddenly he was no
longer on his rooftop: he was in his Hornet roaring
through the skies. He was diving straight down toward
the earth, then at the last minute pulling back up so
that his heart got misplaced to his throat.

Still, he couldn't leave. Spellbound, he watched as
the woman in the garden knelt and began to pull weeds
from her flower beds. While her father dozed, she
worked. The beds emerged little by little, and when
she pulled away a patch of brambles and uncovered
an azalea with a few pitiful blooms clinging to its spin-
dly branches, she danced and twirled with her arms
spread out like wings.

There was celebration in every line of her body,
uninhibited joy over the discovery of one small blooming bush.

The day Bethany had accepted his ring he'd gone

to the florist and picked out five dozen long-stemmed yellow roses, each one as perfect as he'd thought she was. She'd acknowledged them with a small smile and an inclination of her head, like a queen bestowing favors on her adoring public.

The woman danced in her garden until her father woke up. She went to him and tenderly touched his cheek, then wrapped her arms around his waist and guided him back inside.

Jim stayed on the rooftop a long time staring down at the secret garden.

He didn't even know the woman's name, and he wasn't going to ask. As long as she remained anonymous, he could tell himself he was coming to the rooftop for therapeutic purposes, to soak up the sunshine in the daytime and to view the stars at night.

Sarah's new house had five bedrooms, and she didn't settle on the one on the second floor in the west wing until she'd discovered that she could see the Bear's rooftop from her bedroom window. Tonight the Bear was there as still as a mountain, silhouetted by the full moon.

She didn't stop to think what she was doing and why, she merely grabbed her robe and headed out the door. First she checked her father's room to see if he was sleeping, then she raced down the stairs and into the garden.

It was one of those clear evenings when the stars looked close enough to touch, one of those magical nights when fairies danced and moonbeams glowed and dreams sprouted full-blown. In her garden with the lone azalea glowing pink against the brick walls, Sarah dreamed of a time when the garden would be heavy with fragrance and lush with bloom. Walking along its broken brick pathways with her arms folded around herself against the chill, she dreamed of a time when other arms would warm her, another voice would comfort her, another heart would enfold her.

"I'm being a silly romantic," she whispered, glancing upward.

And there he was, the Bear, watching her from afar. Whether it was a trick of the moon or her own imagination, Sarah couldn't say, but light surrounded Jim Standing Bear. He looked like a god that had come down from Mount Olympus.

Her heart stood still. Her legs wouldn't move. Rather than stand in the middle of the pathway gawking, Sarah slid into the shadow of a large crape myrtle tree so that she could watch the Bear, unobserved.

What brought him to the rooftop night after night? Did he notice her? Did the same awareness that made her skin hot ever warm him? Did he know how much she wanted to see his face? To touch him? To hear his voice?

Why had she ducked into the shadow of the trees?

Jim reached for his telescope so he could find her in the darkness, then flung back from it. What was the matter with him? The woman was turning into an obsession.

Instead of sitting on his rooftop like a fool, he should be working on his physical therapy.

He wheeled off the roof and into the elevator, his thoughts murderous. Damn that eighteen-wheeler rig. Damn his legs for not working. Damn Bethany Lawrence for being right.

He *was* a cripple.

The elevator doors swung open, but Jim sat in his wheelchair thinking of a woman in white dancing in her garden.

He couldn't dance.

There was the soft swoosh of doors closing. Jim sat in the dark box of the elevator, thinking about his useless legs.

The doors opened and closed, opened and closed.

He smote his wheelchair with his palms. He was Sioux. The blood of warriors flowed through his veins, the blood of men who had never accepted defeat. Never.

When the doors opened again, Jim went through, bypassing his bedroom and going directly to his exercise room. The parallel bars gleamed in the darkness.

He positioned the wheelchair in front of the bars, then heaved himself upward. Six months of working the weights had made his upper body even more powerful than before the accident.

Getting upright was easy. It was staying there that presented the challenge. His legs quivered.

"Move, damn you. Move."

But they refused. Instead they buckled, and Jim hit the floor like a felled redwood tree.

For a while he lay there panting, and then slowly, ever so slowly, he pulled himself upright once more.

Sarah told herself she was not going to be nosy. She was not going to pry. She was not going to make a complete fool of herself in front of her new housekeeper.

And then she did all three.

"I haven't seen my new neighbor up on his rooftop in a week now," she said. "Is anything wrong?"

Delta put her hands on her hips. "What's wrong with that man would fill a book. He's done hid himself away in that exercise room like some hermit, and if something don't happen soon to bring him out of that shell I don't know what's going to become of him. Lord, I surely don't."

"I'm so sorry," Sarah said, and she meant it.

"Is there anything I can do to help?" she added, meaning that, too. When she'd become a teacher, she sought the jobs nobody else wanted, teaching the kids nobody else would teach, the misfits and rejects, the impoverished, the unwanted, the unloved.

Sarah loved them all.

She missed the children she'd taught and nurtured and loved in La Joya.

"You might try praying, honey. Or you might try taking him a chocolate cake. I ain't never seen Jim Standing Bear resist anything chocolate."

"You think it would be okay?"

Sarah didn't miss the gleam in Delta's eye. She had the look of a meddling woman.

Not that Sarah's motives were all that altruistic. The thought of actually seeing the Bear made her cheeks warm.

"Good neighbors always visit the sick, I say."

"That's what I think, Delta." Her conscience salved, Sarah began to take mixing bowls and cake pans out of the cabinets.

After her cake was finished Sarah went upstairs to dress. Should she wear pink to give her some color or green to match her eyes? Standing in front of her closet she rifled through her dresses. They were all sturdy and sensible. The wardrobe of a schoolteacher. The kind of dresses she could wear and never stand out in a crowd, never be noticed. They were demure, unobtrusive and most of all, wash-and-wear.

Sarah hung the green shirtwaist back in her closet. Who did she think she was trying to fool? She was the proverbial onion in the petunia patch.

Laughing at herself, she ran a hairbrush through her hair without even looking in the mirror, then checked on her father, said goodbye to Delta, got her chocolate cake and headed next door.

There was no sign of life about the house except a small brown car parked in the driveway. Somehow it was not the kind of car she'd expected the Bear to have. A man who did precision flying that thrilled thousands should have a car that cried *daredevil*. A man who had served his country in Strike Fighter Squadron 147 should drive a car that screamed *hero*.

His house was impressive, glass and stucco with perfect landscaping that could only have been done by a professional. Sarah thought it could use a personal touch, though. She preferred a more informal look, a yard that said *somebody loves me*.

If it were up to her she would take out that straight row of boxwoods and put in something that would bear blossoms she could clip off and put in vases around the house. Camellias in all colors and a good tea olive that would perfume the whole yard.

She'd be willing to bet the house could use a homey touch, as well. Say a hand-knit afghan thrown over the back of the sofa and some handwoven baskets to hold magazines and a good cozy mystery or two.

Why, if it were up to her...

A deep blush spread over Sarah's face. What in the world was she doing standing in the Bear's yard fantasizing? Just because she had claimed him as her own rooftop angel didn't mean he was going to invite her in to redecorate, or even to have tea, for that matter.

Why, she'd been out there so long it was a wonder somebody hadn't reported her to the police. Her face still aflame, Sarah hurried to the front stoop and punched his doorbell.

Jim had been at the window when the woman from the garden first appeared in his front yard. Still sweaty from his session with Wayne, his physical therapist, he watched her while Wayne gave an assessment of the day's workout.

Jim was close enough to see that the woman's eyes were as green as the grasses of a spring meadow. Somehow that pleased him.

"With massage we've managed to keep muscle tone in your legs. That's excellent," Wayne said.

The woman was standing in the sunshine looking at his yard as if she planned to redo the whole thing. A little frown creased her forehead and she worried her full bottom lip. Jim smiled.

"Hey, I'm happy about that, too," Wayne said.

Jim didn't bother to correct him. He didn't bother to explain he was smiling because a woman whose name he didn't even know had the most kissable lips he'd ever seen. They were full, lush, and a beautiful shade of rose that had nothing to do with lipstick.

In fact, unless he missed his guess, the woman standing in his yard wasn't wearing a smidge of makeup. The sprinkling of freckles across her nose was all the evidence he needed.

She was fresh and wholesome, the exact opposite of Bethany, who wouldn't have been caught dead without her makeup.

Jim was acutely aware of her. Not merely aware, but vividly interested.

"There's no reason in the world for you not to walk."

The woman's color was suddenly as high as if she'd been caught spying. Fascinated, Jim continued to study her while Wayne's last statement sank in.

Hope can move mountains, but false hope can be a very dangerous thing. Jim knew that firsthand. He'd learned it the hard way this past week, alone in his exercise room with his face kissing the floor.

The woman in the garden was moving toward Jim's front door. He turned away from the window.

"What are you saying, Wayne? That I need a shrink?"

"No, I didn't say that."

The doorbell sliced through Wayne's words, cutting them short. He looked relieved. And in fact, so was Jim. He didn't want to rehash something he'd gone over in his own mind a million times.

"Somebody's at your door."

The woman from the secret garden. The woman who had become an obsession. The woman he couldn't banish from his dreams even after he'd stopped going to the rooftop.

Jim was both elated and terrified. He longed with every fiber of his being to see her face. Just once to look into her eyes. Just for a moment to glimpse the glow of her skin, the sheen of her hair, the graceful column of her neck.

And yet...

He glanced down at his wheelchair, at the legs that used to run for miles without tiring, the feet that used to carry him anywhere he wanted to go.

The doorbell rang again. He couldn't face her.

"Would you get it for me, Wayne?"

"You're sure?"

"Yes. I'm not up to company."

Wayne, who knew his history of reclusivness, started to protest, but one look at the Bear's face sent him to the front door.

Jim heard the door open, heard Wayne's voice. "Yes?"

"Hello, my name is Sarah...Sarah Sloan."

It was a beautiful name, a name Jim hadn't wanted to know. And it was matched by an irresistible, musical voice that drew Jim across the room. He positioned his motorized wheelchair so that he was hidden behind the door but could still have a bird's-eye view of the woman.

"Hello, Sarah. I'm Wayne Wilson."

"Oh...I was hoping...I came to see Jim Standing Bear." Her disappointment was so genuine that Jim felt like a thief. By hiding he'd robbed her of a small pleasure.

"I'm not the Bear. I'm his physical therapist."

"Then that's your car in the driveway?" Sarah's smile transformed her, and Jim wondered why she was so pleased.

He wasn't long finding out.

"No, that's not my car."

"Well, thank goodness...I mean...I just knew the Bear would drive something, oh, I don't know, something wild and romantic."

Wayne was stunned into silence and Jim almost burst out laughing. He couldn't remember when he'd been so entertained. And all because of a woman named Sarah whose honest and simple charm made him forget that her features didn't add up to classic beauty.

In fact, if anybody had asked him to describe her, at that moment he would have said she was the most desirable creature on earth. And she was. With her shining eyes and her high color and her full bottom lip caught between her teeth she was the most delectable woman Jim had ever seen.

A year ago he'd have been doing his damnedest to maneuver her into his bed. He'd have been courting her with every weapon in his arsenal, including a bit of Sioux poetry.

But now all he could do was hide behind a door and watch. He'd always despised cowardly behavior. And now look at him.

"Goodness. Just listen to me. Prattling on like a schoolgirl." Sarah's color deepened. "Perhaps I should start over."

"No, you're doing just fine," Wayne said. "As a matter of fact, I've always found schoolgirl innocence quite charming."

Wayne was actually flirting with Sarah Sloan. Jim wanted to throttle him. He wanted to grab him by the collar and toss him out of the house. He wanted to dare him to ever look at Sarah again, let alone flirt with her.

The intensity of his feelings propelled him from his hiding place. Cursing the slowness of his wheelchair he closed in on Wayne and Sarah. Sarah's eyes widened and Wayne had the grace to look chagrinned.

*Good.* Jim was in a take-scalps mood.

"Thanks for getting the door for me, Wayne. I'll see you next week."

It was clearly a dismissal and Wayne didn't wait

around to say goodbye. With turmoil still roaring through him like a wild river, Jim watched his therapist race down the sidewalk as if rattlesnakes were on his trail.

That's what Jim felt like. A snake. And an ungrateful one, at that. Over the last few months Wayne had withstood Jim's surly moods, his black attitude, and even his rage without ever blinking an eye. Wayne was dedicated, even-tempered and a damned good therapist.

Still, that didn't give him any right to flirt with Jim's woman from the garden. That's how he had come to view her. His personal talisman. When Sarah was in her garden, Jim's own world somehow tilted toward normal. When he saw her digging in the earth, ever hopeful, a tiny glimmer of hope flickered in Jim's heart. However briefly.

And when he saw her dance, he touched the stars once more. *Almost.*

Sarah was his. And nobody was going to take that from him.

She was watching him with equal parts fascination and fear. Why was she afraid?

"Are you..." She bit her lower lip, then started over. "You must be the Bear."

She knew him. It was because of the damned wheelchair, of course.

Sarah Sloan had not come to his house to give him hope: she'd come to offer him pity. Jim's scowl deepened.

What had he been thinking of, leaving his hiding place, exposing himself to the raw emotions of a woman?

"Yes."

His curt reply coupled with his thunderous expression would have sent most women scurrying for cover. It had the opposite effect on Sarah. Her blush and her charming naivete vanished. Nobody would ever have mistaken the strong, self-possessed woman who faced him for a schoolgirl.

"I'm your new neighbor. I apologize for coming over uninvited, but you haven't been coming to your rooftop and I was worried that something might have happened to you."

She looked straight into his eyes, and he felt as if he'd been caught up in the beams of a powerful searchlight. He searched her face and saw not one shred of pity.

Still, Jim couldn't unbend. *Wouldn't* unbend. Embattled warriors never gave an inch. That's how he saw himself, now. Though at the moment he couldn't have said whether his battle was with his wheelchair or the merciless attraction that was turning his blood to fire.

Retreat was out of the question. Attack was his only option.

"As you can see, something *did* happen."

That ought to send her running for the hills.

"I would never have pictured you as a man given to self-pity."

Her remark was like a dash of icy water. It cooled his anger but not his ardor. Damn it all, her courage in the face of his ire only served to stoke the flames that were already raging out of control.

His common sense told him to retreat. His pride told him to stay and fight.

"It's not self-pity you see, Miss Sloan. It's honesty."

"I'm sorry, Mr. Standing Bear. I was out of line, and I sincerely regret that."

She didn't look regretful: she looked like a woman on a mission, though only God knew what it was. If not pity, what? Curiosity? It could be. He'd known folks who were drawn to other people's tragedy, who found a sort of oddball comfort in knowing that fate had caught somebody else in its cross fires and spared them.

Sarah didn't look like that kind of woman. Nor did she appear to be the kind who hung around stage doors and trespassed on private property for a glimpse at somebody the media had made famous.

Beyond Sarah's shoulder a series of contrails mushroomed across the sky. Jim could feel the controls of the jet in his hand, see the gold-tipped clouds as he skimmed their tops. He clenched his jaw and squeezed the arms of his wheelchair so tightly his knuckles turned white.

There was a sound like the strangling of a baby bird, and suddenly Sarah was kneeling beside his chair, one hand on his arm.

"I didn't mean to upset you," she whispered. "Is there anything I can do to help?"

Her touch sent shock waves through him. She was so close he could see the burst of gold in the center of her green eyes. He could smell her hair, her skin. Something soft and floral and utterly enticing.

With color blooming across her cheeks and her head tilted sideways on her slender neck, she reminded him of a rose.

Need became a riptide, swamping him without

mercy, dragging him under. He was drowning in her. *Drowning.*

He had to have air. He had to break free.

"You can leave me the hell alone."

## Chapter Three

Sarah sank into herself, trying to shrivel in her own skin. She felt foolish. Ridiculous. But above all she felt sick at heart. Not for herself. Not because she was embarrassed and uncomfortable and wished she were anywhere except on the Bear's front stoop, wished she were anything except an unwanted guest.

No, she was sick at heart for him, for the proud handsome warrior in the wheelchair who guarded his private grief like the bear he was called, for the dashing pilot who had once soared the skies like an eagle, for the proud hero who had fought for his country without regard for his own well-being.

He deserved better than this. He deserved more than the crippled body, the dashed hopes, the broken dreams.

He was a man of great dignity…and even greater

privacy. Too late she realized her enormous blunder in coming to his house.

She was an intruder. A stranger. She had no right to impose herself upon him. She had no right to bake him chocolate cakes, to speculate about his house and yard, to breach the fortress he'd built around himself.

*Leave,* her mind said, while her heart bade her stay.

He was *her* Bear, her rooftop angel, the man she'd come to rely upon as surely as she relied upon the sun and the moon and the stars. Somehow when he was on the rooftop, everything seemed right with her world. Somehow looking up to see him while she tried to bring order out of chaos reassured her. As long as he was watching over her, she could not be daunted by the tumult in her life. Problems would not overtake her and swallow her soul.

His face was fierce, but *oh,* his eyes... Looking into them, Sarah wanted to brush the lock of black hair from his forehead. She wanted to cradle him against her breast and whisper sweet words that would soothe his soul. She wanted to plant tender kisses all over his face and say, *I understand. I know you don't mean what you said.*

She wanted to hold him, merely to hold him.

His shattered eyes held hers, and the moment became an eternity. She forgot her chocolate cake, she forgot reason, she forgot everything except tenderness.

And something more. Something she dared not explore.

Her hand was still on his arm. She felt the tremor that ran through his body. She sensed that he was on the edge of control.

It was time to go. Past time.

She opened her mouth, but what was there left to

say? Without another word she wheeled around and left his house, left his yard, left her cake sitting on the doorstep like an orphan.

At the hedge between their houses, she turned back to get her cake. Why insult him with unwanted food? He would only construe it as pity.

The Bear was still in his doorway, watching her, his expression as unfathomable as the skies he once claimed as his own.

Riveted, she stood at the hedgerow, prisoner of the fallen warrior, slave to the currents that passed between them. Her breath stalled, her heart stopped beating, her skin caught fire.

She would have stayed there forever for a glimpse of him, merely a glimpse, for somehow in the past thirty minutes he'd gone from guardian angel to obsession, and she didn't know how she was going to live the rest of her life without seeing him. Even from afar.

The sun beat down on her, and her overheated skin felt sticky inside the blue sweater she wore. Perspiration beaded her upper lip and ran down her throat into the collar of her white blouse.

And still the Bear watched her. Something inside her yearned toward him, and even across the distance she felt his response.

Or was she merely dreaming with her eyes wide open?

Abruptly the Bear shut down. The change was as dramatic as if he'd flipped off a light switch. His body stiffened, his expression became guarded, his eyes shuttered.

Loss washed over Sarah. And regret, almost too much regret for a heart to hold.

"Don't shut me out," she wanted to scream.

And yet...Jim Standing Bear was a stranger to her. Everything she knew about him she'd heard from Delta or read in the back issues of the newspaper. She didn't know what kind of breakfast cereal he preferred, whether he liked cream in his coffee, and whether he read the paper before breakfast or afterward. She didn't know if he folded his socks or stuffed them together like sausages. She had no idea of the kind of music he loved, the kind of literature, the kind of pastimes.

Nor would she ever know. Abruptly the Bear wheeled back into his house and closed the front door, shutting out the chocolate cake as surely as he'd shut out Sarah.

Sarah slid through the hedge and back into her own life, a life that was suddenly bereft of magic.

"Did he like that chocolate cake?"

Delta didn't pussyfoot around. If she wanted to know something, even if it was none of her business, she came right out and asked.

Sarah pulled off her sweater and hung it on the coat rack. "I don't know."

"What do you mean? You don't know?" Delta studied her so closely she felt like a bug under a microscope. "Mm-hmm. So that's how it is."

She sounded none too pleased, and all of a sudden Sarah wanted nothing more than to put a pleasant face on the ill-fated visit.

"I barged in without even bothering to call and find out if he wanted company. Goodness, I didn't even bother to find out whether he was free. As it turns out, he was in the midst of a physical therapy session." Sarah got lemonade from the refrigerator and poured two tall glasses, one for herself and one for her dad. "For Pete's sake, I should have known better."

Delta was still scrutinizing her. "Mm-hmm. I see how it is. I most surely do."

Sarah never was good at hiding her feelings. They were always written plainly on her face for the entire world to see. She didn't want Delta or anybody seeing *how it was*.

She could just hear what people would say. *Who does she think she is? Jim Standing Bear wouldn't look twice at a plain woman like her.*

Under the guise of adding cookies to the tray, she turned her back to Delta.

"Is everything all right with Dad?"

"He's right as rain today. Cracking jokes about discovering a cure for Alzheimer's now that he has time on his hands."

Sarah's heart squeezed. Here is where she belonged. At home with the father who needed her. Not running through a hedge to take chocolate cakes to a perfect stranger.

*Perfect.* The word whispered through her mind, but she didn't let herself dwell on it.

"Thank you for watching him while I was gone."

"It wasn't no problem. He's sweet as a lamb."

"I'm going upstairs to take him some lemonade and cookies."

"Why don't you take him out to the garden? The sunshine will do you both good."

Why, indeed? There would be no garden walks for Sarah and her father today. Just in case. In case Jim Standing Bear appeared on his rooftop. In case he glanced her way. In case she glanced his.

In case he could see the small fracture in her heart.

* * *

Sitting just inside the doorway, Jim called himself every kind of bastard. Cruelty was new to Jim. He'd always despised it.

And yet today he'd used it against a sweet woman simply to cover his own inadequacies. He jerked open the door to call her back, to run after her and apologize.

Then he remembered that he couldn't run.

Loss swept through him like winds off the Arctic. He bowed his head, and that's when he noticed the chocolate cake, sitting forlornly on his doorstep.

She'd baked him a cake. His favorite. How had she known? As if he had to wonder. Delta, of course.

He leaned down and scooped the cake up, then carried it into the kitchen. It looked delicious, but Jim had lost his appetite.

The only way he knew to get it back was to apologize to Sarah Sloan. There was no sound in the house except the motor of his wheelchair. No music, no laughter, no sound of friends' voices.

At his desk Jim pulled out a sheet of letterhead stationery. Lt. Cmdr. Jim Standing Bear, U.S. Navy.

He wadded the paper and threw it into the garbage can, then rifled through his desk for something else to write on. A scrap of white paper. Even lined paper would do. Anything except stationery that screamed of the past.

Finally he found a notebook with clean white sheets. Tearing one off, he began to write.

*Dear Ms. Sloan...*

That wouldn't do. It was too formal, too cold. He ripped it up, tore out another sheet and started all over.

*Dear Sarah...*

Jim's hand went still. Even writing her name gave him a perverse thrill.

Taking a deep breath, he started again.

*Thank you for the cake.*

No, that wouldn't do. It sounded as if he were writing a thank-you note. He jerked out another sheet.

*Sarah.*

That was better. Not cold but not so personal, either. No terms of endearment.

*I was unjustifiably cruel to you today, and for that I am sincerely sorry.*

There. That was better.

But how was he going to deliver it? Stamp it and stick it in the mail? Have her sitting in her house for two days thinking him all kinds of monster, thinking herself wrong and foolish for coming to his house?

Jim wadded the note and tossed it into the wastebasket.

There was only one honorable thing to do: apologize to Sarah in person.

It wasn't Fred Astaire who greeted her, but her father, sitting beside the window in a pensive mood.

"I've been thinking, Sarah. It's time for you to go back to work."

"Soon, Dad. I still have a lot of things to do here. Settling in things," she added, but she didn't fool him for a minute.

"I want you and Julie to hire a sitter." His smile was wry. "For my Fred Astaire days."

"Dad, we don't have to talk about this now. I brought cookies and lemonade."

"We have to talk now, Sarah, before Fred comes

back." Laughing, he grabbed a cookie. "Better Fred than King Kong. These are good, Sarah. Have one. You're too skinny."

While she nibbled a cookie, her father pressed his case.

"You know the progression of Alzheimer's. It could take years." He squeezed her hands. "God gave you a talent, Sarah, a beautiful talent for the underdog. Promise me you'll get out of this house and use it."

He tightened his grip on her hands and his voice became urgent.

"Promise me, Sarah."

Here was the man who had been both mother and father to her. The man who had taught her how to skate and how to ride a bicycle and how to look life in the face and dare it to defeat her.

She would do anything for him. Crawl through hell and back if he asked her.

"I promise," she said.

Jim was filled with excitement. And dread. The task ahead loomed large in his mind.

"You don't have to do it. You can pick up the phone and call her."

He was talking to himself. A first. Maybe everybody was right. Maybe his mind was playing dreadful tricks.

Jim couldn't accept that. Day after day he toiled away at the parallel bars. Alone. And day after day he toppled to the floor. Every time.

Apologizing to Sarah in person was a test. If he could do this, then *he* was not the one blocking his progress.

A resolve took hold of Jim. Before he could change his mind, he wheeled through his house and out the front door. The darkness hid him as his wheelchair whirred down the sidewalk.

A sliver of moon rode high in the sky, slipping in and out of the rain clouds that gathered, and only a few stars illuminated the deep black night. What time was it? Too late to call on a neighbor, surely.

Jim was turning back when Sarah's house loomed. His jaw clenched, he steered his chair up her sidewalk. Her house had a porch.

That cinched it. There was no way he could get onto her porch. What was he going to do? Throw rocks at her window?

Jim saw himself as ridiculous. His entire mission was ridiculous.

He was just turning to go when he saw the wheelchair ramp on the side of her porch. Any fool would have guessed that a woman as practical as Sarah Sloan would buy a house with a ramp.

Bumping along the sidewalk, Jim headed for the ramp. He despised the slowness of the chair. He was a man in love with speed, a man accustomed to breaking the sound barrier.

"Don't think about that," he muttered, then struggled up the ramp. He'd made a vow to apologize to Sarah Sloan, and by Custer he was going to do it.

He was sweating by the time he'd reached her front door. He turned his face to the garden to cool off, and that's when he caught a glimpse of white.

Sarah was not in her house; she was in the garden.

Looking at the cumbersome ramp and the long length of lawn that separated him from the garden gate, Jim gave a wry smile.

Apologizing to Miss Sarah Sloan was not going to be easy. He hoped she appreciated his effort. But more than that, he hoped she didn't toss him out on his rump.

"Hellow, Sarah."

The voice sent shivers down her spine. *The Bear*. She looked up from her weeding and found herself staring into the black eyes of the man who had told her to leave him the hell alone.

"I'm sorry if I startled you."

"I don't startle easily. I didn't hear you, that's all."

The moonlight softened his face, made him seem more approachable. But his eyes... They were gleaming obsidian, and they held her with such fierce and tender regard that Sarah couldn't have looked away if her life had depended on it.

She shivered. She felt cold and hot at the same time.

"I came to apologize for my rudeness this afternoon," he said.

"It's quite all right."

"No, it isn't all right."

"I should have called first. I caught you unaware. I'm sorry."

A ghost of a smile played around his lips.

"Do you always do this, Sarah?"

She loved the way he said her name. Like music. Like poetry. Like the soft and insistent beating of native drums.

She licked lips suddenly gone dry.

"Do what?"

"Take the blame. Twist every situation so that you're the one at fault."

"I'm not taking the blame. I'm just stating the obvious. I was out of line coming to your house without calling."

"In that case, I should leave. I didn't call before I came over."

He worked the controls on his chair. In a moment he would be gone and for the rest of her life she would wonder what it would have been like if he'd stayed.

"No, wait. Don't you dare leave, Jim Standing Bear."

He faced her once again, gilded with starlight and laughter. Sarah's heart did a giant flip-flop, and suddenly she saw all kinds of possibilities, such beautiful possibilities she wanted to dance.

"You are the damnedest woman."

"Is that good or bad?"

"It's scary as hell. You scare the hell out of me, Sarah Sloan."

She was as pleased as if he'd given her a dozen roses. She wasn't accustomed to having that effect on men. For that matter, she wasn't accustomed to having any effect at all on members of the opposite sex.

The knowledge that this gorgeous Sioux, this fallen warrior, this dark hero with torture in his soul found her a woman to reckon with made Sarah feel almost beautiful.

Almost.

"I don't usually scare men." She laughed at herself. "Except to scare them away."

There was such poignancy in her voice that Jim caught a glimpse of what Sarah's life must have been like. She was a tall woman. She had probably been a tall child, the kind who would mature slowly, bloom late. She'd probably been gawky as a teenager, her legs too long and skinny, her generous lips too big for her small face. Boys her age would have been too young to see the possibilities, too naive to see beyond the obvious.

Her words haunted him. *I don't usually scare men except to scare them away.*

Life stirred in Jim, and for the first time since his accident he opened himself to emotions. He let himself care, and care deeply.

Sarah must have had second thoughts about revealing so much of herself, for she turned her face away and began to weed her garden once more.

"Sarah." Jim had to lean forward in order to touch her. Tenderly he cupped her face. "Look at me."

Her eyes were enormous, and so clear it was like looking into the deep green waters of the lakes of his childhood. With this woman he felt clean and noble. He wanted to beat his chest, warrior-like. To ride bareback across sweeping plains on a black stallion and take her captive. To cover her with a woven blanket and make her his own.

Looking into her eyes he saw himself as whole. The wheelchair ceased to exist. The accident faded into oblivion. The months of struggle vanished.

There was only Jim Standing Bear, master of the skies and Sarah Sloan, night dancer.

"When I saw you from my window this afternoon standing in the sunshine and checking out my garden with that predatory look on your face…"

"Was I that obvious?" she said.

"…I thought you were the most desirable woman I'd ever seen."

He felt the heat that came into her face. Loved it. Savored it with the tips of his fingers.

Her skin was smooth and soft. Silky. Mesmerizing.

He could have stayed forever in her garden caressing her. Merely caressing her.

"That's not possible," she whispered.

"It's not only possible, it's true."

Her face became radiant, and for a moment she looked like a woman who had always believed in herself, a woman who was accustomed to receiving the adulation of the public, the attention of men.

And yet, Jim knew instinctively that it was not so. Sarah Sloan was a good woman, a strong woman, a caring woman. But she had no idea that she was also a beautiful woman.

"I don't know what to say."

"You don't have to say anything, Sarah. Talk is highly overrated."

A sparkle of laughter burst from her lips, and Jim wanted nothing more than to kiss her. There was a time when he'd have done just that. There was a time when he'd have picked her up and carried her into the house, straight to the nearest bed.

Reality hit him a sledgehammer blow, and he released her. Quickly, before he made a fool of himself.

She was still smiling, her color high.

"You make me feel almost beautiful."

That heartbreaking poignancy was in her voice again. Jim hardened his heart. Who was he to give hope to Sarah Sloan, a man whom hope had abandoned long ago?

She was looking at him with bright expectancy, and Jim silently cursed himself for coming. He should have stayed home. He should have phoned. Hell, he should have mailed the note.

Nice and clean. No entanglements. No expectations. No impossible dreams.

What was there left to say to her? All he could do was stare at her. Stare at her and yearn.

Sarah sensed the change in him immediately.

*Silly goose,* she told herself. He was merely being nice. Flattery probably came easily to a man like him, a man so handsome that he had merely to enter a room for three hundred women to fall into a swoon.

Heat still flooding her cheeks, she turned to the flowerbed and jerked out a handful of weeds, giving herself a pep talk the whole time.

*Get yourself under control. Lighten up. Wise up. Where's that sense of humor that always sees you through?*

Clutching the uprooted weeds, she laughed up at her unexpected visitor.

"If you keep up this flattery I'm liable to end up on your doorstep with another orphan chocolate cake."

There. She'd made him smile.

"Orphan?"

"Yes. I noticed you left my cake sitting on the doorstep."

"I retrieved it. Then ate four pieces."

He liked her cooking. Sarah grabbed elation by the throat and reined it in before she could conjure up images of herself in his kitchen wrapped in a pink apron and up to her elbows in cake batter while the Bear wrapped his arms around her from behind and murmured sweet nothings in her ear.

"Then I shall make you another." She laughed. "Don't look so alarmed. I'll send it over by Delta."

* * *

That was his cue to leave. While he was slightly ahead. Before he made any more bruising mistakes. Caressing her face. Yearning to kiss her. Acting in general like a besotted teenager.

"Take care of yourself, Sarah Sloan."

"You, too, Jim Standing Bear."

Her eyes were impossibly green, like cool river water. And he felt himself drowning.

Jim left quickly, the wheels of his chair bumping over the rough spots, tilting and lurching as if it would spill him out at every turn.

That's all he needed. A tumble out of his wheelchair in front of the woman who already saw him as somebody in need.

He could feel her watching him, feel the heat of her gaze on the back of his neck.

*Don't look back,* he told himself. For he knew that if he looked back, just once, he was lost.

## Chapter Four

The garden was Sarah's refuge. As March gave way to April, Fred Astaire appeared more and more frequently. And he loved dancing, especially in the garden. She was determined to make it a beautiful place for her father, as well as for herself.

Azaleas were in full riot there. Forsythia dripped its golden bells across the garden paths and the early-blooming camellias put on a spectacular show. A star magnolia had burst into full bloom in the northwest corner, surprising Sarah with its pristine beauty.

Wearing a sunhat and a linen wrap to protect her skin, Sarah twirled among the spring blossoms with her father. And that's how Julie found them.

She stood at the garden gate with a picnic basket on one arm and the other lifted to shade her eyes against the sun.

"Hi, I brought us some lunch." She kissed Sarah, then her father. "How are you, Dad?"

He turned to Sarah. "Do I know this beautiful lady, Ginger?"

"It's Julie," Sarah said.

Clicking his heels together and bowing at the waist, he kissed his daughter's hand. "Allow me to introduce myself. I'm Fred Astaire. Do you dance?"

Julie's eyes got misty. "I used to dance with my father, a long time ago."

Sarah squeezed her arm. "It's all right," she whispered. "Everything's going to be all right."

They spread the lunch on an antique cast-iron table Sarah had found at a little shop in the old section of Pensacola.

"Any luck finding a job, Sarah?"

"Yes. One of the teachers at Southside Academy quit, and I'm taking her place, starting next week."

"Southside! No wonder she quit. It's filled with hoodlums and druggies. Couldn't you have found something else?"

"This is what I do, Julie. Work with the kids nobody else wants."

Julie sighed. "You and Dad—always on a mission. You make me feel frivolous, Sarah."

"You're not frivolous, Julie. You have a family to take care of, a wonderful husband and two great children."

"They are great, aren't they? I'll arrange for a sitter to come over after school so I can come here and supervise Dad's new sitter until we're confident she can do the job."

Julie plucked another piece of fried chicken off the

platter. "By the way, your new neighbor was in the news again today. Have you seen the paper?"

"Not yet."

"The Blue Angels are doing a show this weekend in Pensacola."

After Julie left and her dad was settled into his room, Sarah sat down at her kitchen table with a cup of hot tea and the newspaper.

It was all there—Jim Standing Bear's accident, a recap of his career, a quarter page color photo of the Bear in full dress blues standing beside his plane, Number Two of the six F/A-18 Hornets.

The Bear had flown right wing. Now that position was being flown by a twenty-seven-year old aviator from New Jersey.

Sarah traced Jim's picture with the tips of her fingers.

She hadn't seen him since the evening he came to her garden. Not even on his rooftop.

This came as no surprise to her, of course. She'd been right when she told him she never scared men except to scare them away. Apparently Jim Standing Bear was no exception. Which was perfectly all right with Sarah. After all, she had a father to take care of and a household to run and a new job working with children who needed her.

Still…

Sarah sighed. She had more important things to do than daydream. Nonetheless, she got the scissors out of the kitchen desk and clipped the article about the Bear. Then she folded it carefully, carried it upstairs and tucked it into her bedside table.

Jim had discovered that he could see the garden next door from the upstairs library. He'd developed an avid interest in books lately. Not only reading them, but browsing.

It was only natural to glance out the window while he browsed, only natural to stop and admire the flowers blooming next door, only natural to pause when Sarah came into the garden. To be sure she was okay. To be sure she looked happy.

Today she was dancing. Again.

Jim could almost feel the rhythm, almost hear the music. But more than that, he could almost feel Sarah in his arms.

He pressed his fingertips to the windowpane right over the spot where her cheeks glowed pink in the sunshine. Sarah was never more beautiful than when she danced in the garden, her head thrown back, laughing.

Jim watched from the window until the ache in his heart became unbearable. Then he left the library and took the elevator downstairs to his exercise room.

"Torture rack, here I come."

Positioning his wheelchair in front of the parallel bars, he heaved himself upward. He swayed, almost toppled, then regained his balance. This time he stayed upright.

"I will dance again," he said. "I will."

The doorbell jarred Jim awake. He glanced at his bedside clock. One in the morning. It was probably kids, playing a prank.

Pulling the sheet over his head, he rolled over and closed his eyes. The doorbell rang again, persistently this time.

"Ben?"

Jim bolted upright. Something was wrong. Something had happened to his brother. He pulled on his jeans, then struggled into his wheelchair while the bell continued to ring.

Why hadn't somebody called first? Maybe it wasn't about Ben. Maybe somebody had had an accident on the street in front of his house.

"Coming," he called as the doorbell continued to ring.

He jerked the door open and there stood Sarah's father dressed in pajamas and a felt fedora, his feet bare.

"Good evening," he said, smiling. "I thought I'd drop by for a spot of tea."

Jim had never dealt personally with an Alzheimer's patient, but he knew enough about the disease not to argue with Dr. Sloan.

"Won't you come in?" He held the door wide. "Follow me. We'll have our tea in the den."

"How cozy." Dr. Sloan followed him, then hovered in the middle of the room, suddenly uncertain. "Do I know you?"

"I'm Jim Standing Bear, Lieutenant Commander, U.S. Navy."

"Ah, the military. Good people. I've entertained the troops often. Perhaps you've seen me." He held out his hand. "Fred Astaire."

"Won't you sit down, Mr. Astaire? I'll go into the kitchen and brew us a cup of tea."

"A pleasure."

On his way to the kitchen, Jim wheeled by the front door to put the dead bolt on. He didn't want Dr. Sloan to make another escape. Then he went into the kitchen to call Sarah.

She answered on the third ring, her voice still husky with sleep. Husky and decidedly sexy.

"Sarah, this is Jim. I'm sorry to awaken you, but your father is over here."

"Oh, God... Is he all right?"

"Yes, he seems fine. He's sitting in my den waiting for his tea."

"I'll be right over."

"You might want to bring his shoes."

Jim got the teapot from the cabinet, then realized he wasn't wearing a shirt. Too late now. By the time he got upstairs and changed, Sarah would be at his door. Worried. He didn't want to alarm her further by not answering promptly.

No sooner was the thought out of his mind than the doorbell rang.

Sarah was in her gown. It was the old-fashioned kind. Long and white and soft looking. Very feminine. Very appealing.

For a moment Jim forgot to breathe.

"Come in, Sarah. He's in the den."

"I can't thank you enough, Jim. I didn't even know he was missing."

"I started to wait till morning to call, but I thought you might get up in the middle of the night to check on him."

"I usually do."

She followed him into the den. Her father was stretched full-length on the sofa, his hat still on, fast asleep.

"Oh, my God."

Sarah knelt beside him and gently removed his hat. Then she smoothed his hair. The tender gesture tore at Jim's heart.

"He looks so peaceful it's a shame to wake him," she whispered.

"Then don't. Let him sleep."

Jim retrieved an afghan from the closet and handed it to Sarah, lingering over the small task. His hand brushed hers. Accidentally? Deliberately?

Shock waves went through him and her eyes widened. Catching her full lower lip between her teeth, she turned back to the sofa to cover her dad.

Still, Jim didn't move away. He couldn't, for Sarah smelled like roses and he was trapped in the heavenly fragrance, trapped in the nearness of her.

"I still can't believe it." Sarah smoothed the afghan over her father, and her hands began to tremble. "What if he hadn't come here? What if he had wandered into the street and gotten killed?"

"He didn't. He's safe now, Sarah."

"Oh, God..."

Sarah turned to him and there were tears in her eyes. Jim didn't stop to reason. He didn't pause to think about consequences or propriety.

Leaning down he scooped her onto his lap. She didn't protest, didn't express surprise. She merely curled into him like a kitten, pressed her face into his bare chest and cried.

"There, there," he murmured, smoothing her silky hair. "Let it all out. I'm here."

"This is so weak. To cry."

Her statement was muffled and jerky, punctuated by sobs. With one arm around her waist, the other woven in her hair Jim drew her closer.

He was in heaven. He was in hell.

"You're not weak. You're the bravest woman I know."

She cried even harder.

"I can't...I can't seem to stop."

"That's all right. Cry as long as you like."

He didn't want her to stop. Selfish bastard that he was, her anguish gave him a perfect excuse to hold her. No, not merely hold her. To caress her.

He smoothed her hair, rubbed her back, ran his arms up and down the length of her arms. She was soft and fragrant and altogether enchanting.

But more than that, she was desirable. As her sobs began to subside, she adjusted her weight. Desire stabbed him with a force that shook Jim.

Over the last few months he'd wondered if he would ever feel passion again. Not because of Bethany's desertion. It had taken him a surprisingly short while to get over her.

No, not because of Bethany, but because of his own condition. Crippled. Confined to a chair. Dependent for months on pills to kill the pain.

There was no doubt about his condition now. His arousal was obvious...and impossible to hide.

What would Sarah think?

"You are so kind," she murmured, her warm breath whispering against his skin.

*Kind* is not the word he would use to describe himself, especially not at the moment.

"I don't know what I would have done if I had awakened to find my father gone. Jim..."

She lifted her face to his, and her voice trailed away. Awareness leaped into her eyes. Jim held his breath.

And then...

Her arms stole around his neck and his lips claimed hers and he was kissing her and she was kissing him back. It was a miracle. Miracles happened only once in a lifetime, and Jim knew better than to question this one.

Her lips were lush. Delicious. He couldn't get enough of them. He couldn't get enough of her.

She shifted. He tightened his hold. Her full breasts were pressed enticingly into his bare chest. Separated from her only by the thin fabric of her gown, he felt how her body responded to him. She ripened and bloomed, as rich and lush as the garden she tended so carefully.

Her lips parted in sweet invitation, and he explored her honeyed depths. The sensual play of tongues ignited a fire in his blood. He'd kissed her a thousand times in his dreams, but nothing had prepared him for the real thing.

Sarah wove her fingers in his hair and pulled him closer. Time suspended. Place vanished. There was only the two of them, caught up in a passion that raged like a wild river.

Every inch of his body was sensitized. Her slightest movement caused a friction that spurred his desire.

Sarah was not a silent lover. She allowed an intensity of feeling to rock her. She moaned and swayed against him, her aroused nipples brushing across his chest with an erotic friction that almost shattered his control.

Locked in the tight confines of the wheelchair, their bodies were as intimate as if they were making love.

*Almost.*

Every fiber in his being yearned to love her, fully, completely. His exultation was in knowing that it could happen. His private hell was in knowing that he could only be a passive recipient.

Sarah deserved more. She deserved a man who

could savor her in every conceivable way, no holds barred.

Jim became aware of the clock ticking off the minutes, of Sarah's father who lay sleeping nearby, of the wheelchair that bound him as surely as chains.

Who did he think he was fooling? Sarah was kissing him out of gratitude. Nothing more.

He didn't need her charity. If she came to him...*when* she came to him, it would be with desire and need and the absolute certainty that Jim Standing Bear was whole.

Sarah felt the change in Jim immediately. He simply shut down. One minute he was kissing her as if he'd invented it specifically for her, and the next he was as remote as Mount Everest.

And just as unattainable.

She could die. That was all. If a big hole would open up in the middle of the room, she'd jump right in and pull it in behind her.

He must think her a depraved fool, coming to his door in her nightgown, practically drooling all over him at the sight of his bare chest, wallowing in his lap like a wanton.

And with her father sleeping on the couch, for Pete's sake. Lord, if Jim hadn't gone cold all of a sudden, what would she have done?

Made love to him right there in plain view of God and her own father. That's what she would have done. The Bear did that to her—made her forget propriety, made her forget common sense, made her forget everything except the magnificent fallen warrior who could turn her to a quivering mass of hormones. Pheromones, too, she guessed.

He ended the kiss, ended her fantasies, ended her

life, it seemed. She was still pressed up against him in a manner worthy of the floozies she'd seen on Bourbon Street in the French Quarter. She could feel the beat of his heart. Her only consolation was that it was thundering as hard as hers.

Runaway hearts. What was that a sign of? Excitement? Passion? Fear? Embarrassment?

That had to be it. He was as embarrassed as she.

"Jim."

That's all she could say, for her heart was too full to speak.

"Sarah."

If eyes could talk his would be speaking volumes. She saw pain there. And confusion.

She climbed out of his lap and smoothed her gown, then her hair.

"You must think I'm awful," she whispered. "I don't know what came over me."

"It was my fault. I apologize, Sarah."

Oh, God, he was *apologizing* for kissing her. She died all over again.

"It won't happen again," he said. "I promise you."

That was even worse. Here she was wishing he would kiss her again. Immediately. And hard. And he was making promises that sliced her heart like knives.

"Well, of course not," she said. "Sometimes people do rash things when they are upset. And I was upset."

He reached toward her, then quickly withdrew his hand and backed away, putting the distance of the room between them.

"Are you okay now, Sarah?"

"Yes. I'm perfectly all right."

It was an outright lie. How could a woman like her

be okay when a man like Jim Standing Bear walked out of her life? Figuratively, of course, for the Bear couldn't walk at all.

Suddenly Sarah saw the problem clearly. It was the wheelchair that stood between them. She wanted to race across the room and beat her hands on his gorgeous chest. She wanted to scream, "Don't you know it doesn't matter?"

Instead she kept her distance, and he kept his dignity. She owed him that.

"Thank you, Jim. For everything."

"You're welcome."

So formal. So polite. As if they were complete strangers.

"I'll just wake Dad up and we'll be leaving."

"There's no need to do that. This house is huge. You can stay here the rest of the night."

"We've imposed on you enough."

"You don't need to be out there in the middle of the night with Dr. Sloan. You should stay."

"I'll just put his shoes on, and we'll go."

She knelt beside the sofa to retrieve the shoes she'd brought over, and suddenly Jim was beside her, his hand on her arm. His touch sent shock waves all the way to her toes.

"Stay, Sarah. I insist."

"All right, then. We'll stay. It's probably best for Dad."

Selfishness made her say yes. And then to compound her crime, she used her father as an excuse. But with the touch of Jim's hand on her arm and the feel of his kiss still on her lips, how could she have said no?

Besides, this would be her once-in-a-lifetime opportunity to sleep in Jim Standing Bear's house. Perhaps in a bed where he had slept. Maybe even using the same covers. She liked to think so. She liked to imagine that a quilt that had lain intimately against the Bear's skin would caress her own. Even for a little while.

"Anyhow," she said, "it'll be dawn before we know it. I'll just cuddle up in that comfortable-looking chair by the fireplace and we'll be gone before you wake up in the morning."

"No." His face was so fierce Sarah cringed. "With dead bolts on every door, your father is perfectly safe here in the den. Most of the bedrooms are upstairs, but there's one downstairs if that makes you more comfortable."

"Downstairs will be fine."

His hand was still on her arm. His eyes were still searching her face.

"Sarah..."

The long silence was heavy with things they couldn't say. But, oh, there was so much in a look.

Finally Jim released her, and she knew that long after she went to bed she would ponder this moment.

"I can stay down here and keep watch if that will make you feel better about your father."

"No."

Her eyes slid to his wheelchair. She knew the minute they did that it was a mistake. The cold formality came over him once more. She tried to correct her error.

"You said the house is secure, so I won't worry. Honestly, I won't."

"That's it, then. The bedroom is down the hall to

the right. You'll find everything you need in the closet.''

Abruptly he left the room, pausing only long enough in the doorway for a curt *good night.*

''Good night,'' she whispered. ''Sweet dreams, my wounded warrior.''

But there was no one to hear.

## Chapter Five

Jim knew he wouldn't sleep. He didn't even try. Instead he sat upstairs in his bedroom listening to the sounds a house makes at night and waiting for the sunrise.

As soon as the first light hit his window, he put on a clean shirt and went downstairs. Dr. Eric Sloan was still asleep on the sofa. That meant Sarah was still there. In Jim's house. In his bed. Sleeping under the blanket his grandmother had woven, the symbol of Earth Mother resting across her breasts and the symbol of Father Sky spreading his fertility upon her womb.

The image stayed with him in the kitchen while he made coffee. If he couldn't have her, at least he could have the vision.

At least he could have a memory of her sitting across from him at the kitchen table with the early morning sun in her hair. Jim poured himself a cup of coffee, then set about making breakfast.

"I smell bacon."

Dr. Sloan stood in the doorway, his pajama top askew, his hat perched on his head.

"Good morning," Jim said, and then he reintroduced himself in case the doctor didn't remember.

"I know who you are, young man. The question is, do you know how to cook? The bacon's burning."

With that Dr. Sloan went to the stove and picked up the long-handled fork. Jim was scared he would set the house on fire.

"Here, let me do that."

"Stand back, young man. I've been cooking for thirty-something years. Why, when Sarah was a baby..."

A frightened look came into the old man's eyes, and he sat heavily on a nearby stool.

"Where am I?"

"In Pensacola at the home of your next-door neighbor." Jim introduced himself once more, including his naval rank. "You and Sarah were my guests for the evening."

"Where's Sarah?"

"Still asleep, I believe. In the bedroom next to the den where you slept."

"I see." A look of unutterable sadness came into Dr. Sloan's face.

"What I hate most about this disease is what it does to my daughters, especially Sarah. She's a caretaker, you know. She's always been that way. Even when she was a child."

His eyes misted over.

"She makes sacrifices," he added. "Too many sacrifices."

Dr. Sloan looked at Jim with such intense scrutiny he felt as if he were under a microscope.

"What is Sarah to you?"

"A neighbor, a friend, and a very attractive woman."

"You'll have to forgive my bluntness, Lieutenant Commander. These moments of lucidity come so infrequently I have to say all the important things while I can. I don't want Sarah to be hurt."

"I won't hurt her, Dr. Sloan," Jim answered. "I can promise you that. And I can also promise you that she will never sacrifice herself for me."

"You said you were her friend."

"That's true."

"If she needs you, will you be there for her? I'm not talking about all these modern-day catch phrases like emotional support. I'm talking about *real* ways."

"You have my word."

"You strike me as the kind of man who doesn't give his word lightly."

"No, sir."

Dr. Sloan's eyes twinkled as he clasped Jim's shoulder. "I think the two of us are going to get along fine, even when I'm Fred Astaire."

Sarah didn't mean to be eavesdropping, but she had been on her way to the kitchen and had arrived in time to hear her father coercing Jim Standing Bear into being her friend.

She had to let him off the hook.

"You two have the guilty look of plotters."

Jim looked chagrined and her father laughed. Sarah moved into the kitchen.

"Don't mind a word he says, Jim. He's being the overprotective father. As usual." She leaned over and kissed her father on the cheek. "Morning, Dad. Glad you're back."

"Me, too."

To Jim she said, "I found this robe in the closet. I hope you don't mind."

"Not at all. It looks better on you than on me."

So, it was his robe, after all. Sarah had thought so. She'd hoped so.

She belted the robe tighter and unconsciously snuggled closer. It was almost like being hugged. The scent of him lingered in the terry-cloth folds, something woodsy and fresh. She hoped his scent soaked into her skin and stayed there for days. Weeks. Months.

Forever.

"Coffee?"

Jim's eyes were bloodshot, as if he hadn't slept a wink. Still, there was a fire in their depths that held her captive. She couldn't have looked away if her life had depended on it.

"Yes, please."

His hand touched hers, lingered there, struck an answering fire in her blood. Sarah came gloriously, wondrously alive, and for a moment she saw herself as beautiful, desirable, a woman to be reckoned with.

"We're making breakfast. I hope you can stay."

Jim withdrew to the stove. Deprived of his touch and the flame in his eyes, she reverted to plain Sarah with sleep-puffed eyes and straight unimaginative hair and the face that would never launch a thousand rubber duckies, let alone a thousand ships.

"Yes, thank you. We'll stay."

Selfish witch that she was, she would do anything to prolong contact with him.

Breakfast turned out to be not only stimulating but fun. With Jim sitting across the table from her, she could ogle all she pleased without being obvious.

Fortunately, her father stayed with them through the meal. Always a great raconteur, Dr. Sloan carried the conversation, regaling Jim with tales from the years spent in Mexico.

Was it her imagination, or did Jim perk up every time her father mentioned her name? Sarah was sorry to see the meal come to an end.

"We have to be going, Dad."

She started to remove Jim's robe. He put a hand on her shoulder to stop her.

"No. Keep it. You'll need it walking home."

"Thank you, Jim. For everything."

Would he catch her double meaning? Would he understand she was talking about the kiss?

If he did, he didn't let on.

"I'll be seeing you, Sarah," he said, and then he escorted them to the door.

Back at home in her bedroom, Sarah pressed her face into his bathrobe and cried.


Jim didn't know which was worse: the torture of not having Sarah in his house, or the torture of seeing the jets. F/A-18 Hornets. The Blue Angels. Flying fast and high. Thrilling the crowd. Owning the skies.

He closed all the curtains then went to his exercise room and turned the radio up loud.

Then he took up the challenge of the parallel bars. He knew the routine: Drag himself upright. Fall. Pull up again. Tumble. Up and down. Again and again, until sweat beaded his upper body and fatigue trembled his lower. Until walking seemed an illusion, and dancing an impossible dream.

Mac Thompson, the principal of Southside Academy, was a seasoned, no-nonsense educator who cared deeply for two things—the students in his school and the teachers who worked with them. He looked over the tops of his wire-rimmed glasses at Sarah.

"The first thing I want you to know, Miss Sloan, is that Southside Academy is the stepchild of the school district. Our budget barely covers the basics. The school board thinks it best to spend money on the children that matter, and to them, the kids at Southside don't matter. In the opinion of our esteemed board, these kids have already fallen through the cracks."

"They matter to me, Dr. Thompson."

"Good." He smiled for the first time since she'd entered his office.

"Miss Sloan, this is not going to be easy."

"I understand, Dr. Thompson. As you know from my resume, I've had experience with children like these."

"The class you're going into is all boys—adolescent boys, full of hormones and trouble. Here's the class roster."

He passed a file folder to her. "Take a look. Mohammed and Jared and Thomas are in drug rehab. Sampson already has a police record. Archie tried to stab his father. The other five are the best of the lot, and not a one of them can read above a third-grade level."

Behind Mac Thompson's glasses gleamed the eyes of a crusader. "Grace Barnes couldn't handle them. Do you think you can?"

Sarah's chin came up a notch. "I *know* I can."

"Good." Mac Thompson stood up. "Follow me. I'll lead you to the lion's den."

Mac Thompson's description of Sarah's new classroom was accurate. As soon as the principal disappeared her *lions* bared their teeth. They lobbed her with spitballs, they minced around her making lewd remarks, they threw chalk, they refused to open books.

Sarah was not daunted. She faced them, smiling.

"I am not Grace Barnes," she said. "I won't leave."

"You sure ain't. You got a great a—"

"Archie." Sarah's voice cut through his like a whip. She went to his desk and stood face to face with the offender. Actually face to chest was more like it. Archie towered over her.

"Come with me," she said.

"I ain't going to no principal's office."

"No, you're not," she said gently. "We're going up front to read."

The rest of the class burst out laughing. Sarah smiled sweetly at them.

"And so are the rest of you. Follow me, gentlemen."

"Miss Sloan, you must be in the wrong classroom," the one called Sampson said. "There ain't no gentlemen here."

"No," she smiled at them. "I'm in exactly the right place. And before the school year is over, there *will* be gentlemen here."

* * *

"How did it go?" Julie asked when Sarah got home.

"They declared war, and I'm fighting back."

"That's awful."

"No, it's wonderful. Apathy would be awful. They want somebody to *look* at them, somebody to care." Sarah hung her sweater in the closet. "How's the new sitter?"

"She seems nice enough, but..." Julie's voice trailed off.

"But what?"

"There's nothing I can put my finger on, but she seems so *bland*. And Dad seems depressed. He kept asking, 'Where's Ginger?' God, how do you endure it, Sarah?"

"Don't make me a saint, Julie. I'm not."

"But you're so...together. You always have been. I've envied that, you know."

Julie had it all—husband, children, friends, beauty, personality. Her admission shocked Sarah to the core. If anybody had reason to envy, it was she.

Sarah put her arms around her sister. "Go home, Julie. Your children need you."

"I'll come back tomorrow, just to be sure about that sitter."

"Fine, See you then."

After Julie left, Sarah glanced up the stairs. She should check on her dad. She should let him know that *Ginger* was here. She should see for herself how the sitter was doing.

And she would. But first she had to replenish her soul, buoy her spirit.

She went into the kitchen and made herself a cup

of hot tea, then carried it up to her private suite. The yellow room always looked as if it were smiling, especially when it was filled with sunlight. The late afternoon sun danced off the walls and fell across the robe that lay on Sarah's bed.

Jim's robe. Setting her tea on the bedside table, she stretched across the bed and buried her face in the robe, inhaling his scent. Memories swamped her, and Sarah closed her eyes.

The Bear had kissed her as no man ever had. He had kissed her in the way of a man who loves a woman.

She knew she was being a foolish romantic. She knew she was clinging to impossible dreams. Still, without dreams the spirit would die. She knew that.

Suddenly, Sarah sat bolt upright.

"That's it!"

Her children, the misfit boys at Southside Academy, needed a dream. And she knew how to give it to them.

Leaving her tea to get cold, she hunted through the telephone book for Jim Standing Bear's number. It took five rings for him to answer. By the time Sarah heard his voice she was trembling like a leaf.

"Hello." His voice sent chills over her.

"Jim, this is Sarah."

"Sarah." Was that pleasure she heard in his voice, or was she dreaming? "Is everything all right? How's your dad?"

"Yes, to the first question. He's fine, to the second." Sarah laughed with the pure joy of talking to him. "But there is something I'd like to talk to you about."

"Certainly."

"Not on the phone. In person."

Silence. Was he going to refuse to see her? Sarah plunged boldly ahead.

"I'd like to come over, if it's all right with you."

"When?"

"Now? The sitter's with Dad, and I...I really should bring your robe home. I meant to do it yesterday."

"That's not a problem."

He paused. Was he going to turn her down?

"Come on over, Sarah. I'll be waiting for you."

Sarah set the receiver back in its cradle, then fisted the air in victory.

"Yes!"

She pressed the intercom to her father's room. The sitter responded immediately. Sarah took that as a good sign.

"Mrs. Grimes, this is Sarah. Is everything all right down there?"

"Yes. Dr. Sloan is napping."

"Good. I'm going next door. I'll see you when I get back."

"How long will you be gone?"

How long would it take to tell Jim her plan? Fifteen minutes. Max. Suppose he kissed her again?

Her face bloomed pink at the thought.

"I don't really know, Mrs. Grimes. All I can tell you is that I'll be home before you leave at six."

Sarah was halfway down the staircase before she remembered Jim's robe. She raced back to get it, and by the time she arrived at his house she was breathless from exertion. Or so she told herself.

The minute he answered the door, she understood that her condition was due to something else entirely. Her condition was due to the excitement of seeing him, an anticipation almost too great for the heart to bear and a skin-searing, blood-boiling passion that stole the starch from her bones.

"Hello, Sarah," he said, and she melted like a stick of butter that had been left too long in the sun. "Won't you come in?"

Was that spark she saw in his eyes *interest?* She pinched herself to be sure she was wide-awake. Then she had to pinch herself again, for Jim Standing Bear was leading her into his den, back to the place where it all had happened.

Sarah stood in the doorway while memories rendered her speechless. There was the sofa where her father had slept, and there was the rug where she'd knelt when Jim lifted her onto his lap and kissed her. There was where she'd beheld magic.

Jim tossed the robe over the back of the sofa.

"Won't you sit down, Sarah?"

That was a good sign, wasn't it? She sat beside his robe close enough to touch, then surreptitiously buried the fingers of her right hand in its soft folds. To give her courage.

Jim felt at a disadvantage in his wheelchair. If he were having a discussion with Ben or Wayne or any other man, he'd have swung himself into a wingback chair.

But he wouldn't do that while Sarah watched. Being in the condition was bad enough without calling her attention to it.

"I was never a woman to beat about the bush, Jim, so I'll get right to the point."

That was one of the things he liked about Sarah. No pretense. No posturing.

He would have thought she was perfectly at ease if he hadn't seen how she clutched the robe. Jim smiled.

"I'm listening, Sarah."

Her tongue flicked over her bottom lip, another sure sign that the unflappable Miss Sarah Sloan was not as composed as she seemed.

"My father always used to say that. When Julie or I were children and would go to him with a problem, he'd pull us onto his lap and say, 'I'm listening.'"

"If it will make you feel more comfortable, I'll pull you onto my lap."

"Not unless you want this meeting to take a while. As I recall, the last time you did that, we got sidetracked."

They stared at each other, astonished at their audacity, astonished at the easy way they'd slipped into such familiarity, almost as if they were lovers.

Jim felt as if he were flying a jet off the deck of an aircraft carrier. Once a pilot committed the plane to takeoff, there was no turning back.

And it felt good. He felt a freedom he hadn't felt in months.

He held Sarah's gaze, loving the way her flush deepened, loving the way she crossed her legs, then uncrossed them and tugged at her skirt. Then crossed them again.

"I'm getting sidetracked now," he said.

"So am I."

If he hadn't been in his wheelchair he'd have strode across the room and pulled her into his arms. He'd have kissed her until they were both breathless, kissed her until kissing wasn't enough, kissed her until the only possible way to satisfy their hunger was upstairs in his king-sized bed.

"Oh, dear," she said, as if she'd read his thoughts.

She pushed her hair back from her flushed face, then laughed. A bit self-consciously, he thought. He hoped.

"Some get-right-to-the-point person I turned out to be."

"I liked your digression."

"Did you?"

"Absolutely. I haven't felt playful in a long time. You make me feel playful."

"And you make me feel…" She flushed again.

"How do I make you feel, Sarah?"

"Beautiful. Almost."

There it was again. Sarah Sloan's Achilles heel. Jim wheeled his chair across the room and leaned over to cup her face.

"You *are* beautiful, Sarah."

He felt how she trembled at his touch. He reveled in it, loved it.

He wanted to kiss her. But not here. Not now. Not while he was still imprisoned by the wheelchair.

Her eyes were wide and misty. Sarah Sloan had the look of a woman who expected to be kissed.

Jim silently berated himself for being a selfish bastard. He had no right to touch her.

And yet… His hands were on her face, and she was watching him with a misty-eyed look that tore his heart in two. How could he bear to pull away?

Fortunately, Sarah saved him. She drew back and covered her embarrassment by rearranging her skirt. Silently, Jim wheeled back across the floor.

"Oh, my goodness. I came here for the children. Not this."

"The children?"

"Yes, my students. At Southside Academy."

He was familiar with Southside. He could picture Sarah there bringing her strength and honesty and caring spirit to those lost souls who had been booted out of the traditional school system.

"You've taken on quite a challenge, Sarah."

"I like challenge."

So did he. The realization pleased Jim. There were still parts of him that the accident hadn't destroyed.

He waited for her to continue.

"My students are all boys, Jim. Adolescents who have fought against society in every way possible, defiance, drugs, even crime."

This was an aspect of the school he had never considered. His blood chilled at the idea of Sarah being in danger.

"Does the school provide security for its teachers, Sarah?"

"Absolutely. They provide all the security the teachers need. But little else, Jim. When the budget pie is sliced, Southside is generally overlooked. My students need equipment, books, supplies.

"But most of all they need a hero, and that's where you come in."

"You're talking to the wrong person, Sarah."

"No, I'm talking to exactly the right person, Jim. I want you to come to Southside and mentor these troubled adolescent boys. Two days a week, Jim. That's all I'm asking."

"I can give you a list of people who can do that for you. Commander Chuck Sayers, for one. I think he'd be happy to carve out some time for your worthy cause."

"This is not a cause, Jim. It's a crusade. I'm sure Commander Sayers is a great guy, but I need someone who can donate more than a little time. I need some-one who will be committed to these boys.''

She fell silent, giving her speech time to sink in.

''I need you, Jim.''

He needed her, too, but not in the way she was describing.

''My answer is no.''

He could tell by the way she stiffened her spine that she wasn't going to take *no* for an answer.

''Why?''

''That should be obvious.''

''No, it's not. Explain.''

''In the first place, I'm no hero, Sarah. I'm merely a man who served his country as thousands of men and women have before me, and will after me.''

''You're a Blue Angel.''

''I *was* a Blue Angel.''

''You're still a celebrity, Jim. Somebody people re-member and admire, somebody these young boys could pattern themselves after.''

''I'm confined to a wheelchair, Sarah.''

''No, Jim, you're imprisoned by your wheelchair.''

The flush on her cheeks was no longer passion; it was anger. She jumped up from the sofa and paced his den like an avenging angel.

''All right, have it your way. I'm in prison.''

''One of your own making.''

''If your intent is to provoke me to anger, you're dong a hell of a job.''

Two feet from him, she stopped pacing and stood glaring with her arms akimbo.

''Let me tell you about a little five-year-old boy in Mexico. He pushed himself around by hand in a makeshift wooden platform that had cast-off wheels from a rusty pair of roller skates. He had no legs, Jim.''

She started pacing again, gesturing as she talked. ''He was one of my students in La Joya, and he entered every race we had at school. He never won, but that didn't keep him from trying.

''Another of my students was a little girl who was born without fingers. She taught herself to hold a pencil between her stumps. She wanted to be an artist.''

Sarah glanced at him, expecting a comment. Jim was silent. Waiting. Listening.

''I had a five-year-old boy with only one ear, a six-year-old girl with Down's Syndrome. They lived in shacks made of cardboard and rusty tin and whatever bits of wood they could find. They kept goats and chickens in the yard and when they bathed it was in a barrel outside.''

Her voice softened, and she stood in front of him once more, her eyes shining with tears.

''Every Sunday they walked up the steep mountain path to a pavilion with a primitive cross attached to the top and they sat in a circle on the concrete floor and told of all the things they had to be thankful for. And when they sang, you could hear their voices lifted in praise all the way down the mountainside.''

The tears slid down her cheeks, glistening on her soft skin, and Jim had to grip the arms of his wheelchair to keep from reaching up and wiping them away.

''You're a good woman, Sarah Sloan. The world would be a better place if there were more people like you.''

Sarah stared at him, making no attempt to check the tears that continued to flow.

''And like you, Jim Standing Bear.''

"Don't pin any medals on me."

"I won't. Not until you prove yourself."

Jim smiled. "You're stubborn, too. You're going to stand there and badger me, aren't you?"

"I'm going to do whatever it takes. I'll stand here till hell freezes over if it takes that long to convince you to share yourself with my boys at Southside."

"How long have you been there, Sarah?"

"One day."

"And they're already *your* boys?"

She flushed. "Yes. It doesn't take me long to make up my mind about people."

Jim grinned. "Lucky me. Today was my day to be chosen."

Smiling through her tears, she swiped at her face with the back of her hand.

"Lucky you. Say *yes,* Jim."

"What exactly would I be saying *yes* to?"

"I thought you were the kind of man who believed in taking risks."

"I used to be." His smile was rueful. "I guess I still am. All right, Sarah. You've won. I surrender."

"Yes!" Sarah made her hoorah sign in the air with her right fist, then without thinking she wrapped her arms around Jim.

He was a mountain, the Rock of Gibraltar, the rock of ages, a fortress that she clung to for the sheer joy of being there.

"You've made me so happy," she whispered.

"I'm glad."

Then slowly, ever so slowly his arms stole around her, and he was hugging her back.

More than hugging. He was caressing her, her arms,

her back, her hair, and Sarah was in heaven. She closed her eyes and sighed. She couldn't help it. Sometimes paradise came so quickly it took her breath away.

She felt the thunder of his heart against hers, smelled the clean outdoorsy scent of his skin. She could have stayed in his arms forever.

Guilt slashed her. The sitter was waiting for her, and her father was sitting upstairs in his bedroom in the lonely isolation of his disease.

"I really should go," she murmured.

For a heartbeat he held her closer, then he released her. Sarah smoothed her blouse and pushed her hair back from her flushed face, and the Bear watched her with eyes as dark and unfathomable as the bottom of the ocean.

If he apologized for caressing her, she was going to start screaming and never stop.

He didn't, and she took a ragged breath.

"I brought a file folder on the children for you to get acquainted with them. Then we'll need to talk again, perhaps tomorrow in the garden over a cup of tea?"

He was so still she thought he was going to refuse. She thought he was going to change his mind about helping her boys.

"I have a better idea. Why don't you come over tomorrow after school and we'll go to the beach? I know the perfect spot for talking."

Sarah flew home on wings.

"Yes," she'd told him. "Yes!"

Her feet didn't touch the ground till she came to the long winding staircase that would carry her upstairs to her father.

## Chapter Six

They loaded the picnic lunch into Jim's specially equipped van, and he drove them to a section of beach secluded by sand dunes piled head high and a thick stand of sago palms.

A sagging volleyball net was slung between two poles weathered gray by wind and rain and time, and in the distance dolphins leaped silver in the surf.

Sarah spread Jim's Indian blanket, then kicked off her shoes before sitting cross-legged and serving up heaping plates of potato salad, ham sandwiches, apples and cheese.

She was a barefoot goddess in the sun. Jim could hardly concentrate on the food.

"This looks delicious," Sarah said.

"It certainly does."

He was looking directly into her eyes, and she flushed pink at his remark. He wanted her more than any woman he'd ever known. He ached for her in ways that brought sweat to his brow.

Jim broke eye contact. "Delta outdid herself," he said.

"I'll have to remember to thank her."

Jim busied himself with the food, avoiding eye contact as much as possible. That's all it took for him— one glance and he was swamped by such longing it made his heart hurt.

After they'd finished eating, Sarah gathered the remainders of their picnic, then arranged herself on the blanket and smiled up at him.

"I think what you will be able to do for my boys is wonderful. How can I ever thank you, Jim?"

"You already have."

"I have? How?"

"When you kicked off your shoes and smiled as if you'd found paradise. That's thanks enough for any man."

Emboldened by his choice of words, she stretched full length on his blanket with her arms folded behind her head.

"I've found paradise." She smiled up at him. "Why did you choose this place, Jim?"

"Because of the dolphins. I used to come here on my days off. I could spend hours watching them and wondering what they know that we don't know."

"Do you think they have a language, Jim?"

"I'm no marine biologist, but my answer is yes. Furthermore, I think the day will come when we can communicate with them."

Sarah sat up and buried her toes in the sand. "This feels so good."

"Yes, I remember."

His poignant answer tore at her heart. Sarah didn't stop to analyze, didn't pause to rationalize. For once in her life she merely *acted*.

She reached for his shoelaces, and Jim made a sound very much like the grizzly whose name he bore.

"Let's live dangerously, Jim."

She kept her tone light, but her heart was hammering so hard she wondered that he didn't hear.

She hated the way her hands shook as she untied his shoes. She felt like an imposter, a country bumpkin all dressed up and pretending to be a sophisticated lady.

She pulled off his shoes and set them on the blanket. He was wearing athletic socks, blindingly white and so masculine they made her mouth dry.

Dear Lord in Heaven, what was she doing?

Jim was so still he might have turned into a stone statue. She didn't dare look at his face. What was he thinking?

What was *she* thinking?

*Don't think. If you do you're lost.*

She peeled his socks away, lingering over the task, loving the way his body heat transferred itself to her hands, then to her heart.

There was a long low sound like the rumble of thunder. Jim shuddered, and Sarah felt the vibrations in the palms of her hands.

His feet were long and graceful, copper-colored and intensely masculine. Sarah's fingers paled against his skin. Her palms grew damp. Chills made goose bumps rise on her arm, then she felt so hot she wanted to cast off all her clothes and run into the sea screaming.

Or into his arms. Definitely into his arms.

Reason flew straight up to the skies to join the circling seagulls. All Sarah knew was that she couldn't let go.

She traced the line of veins that criss-crossed his arch. Then she made a circle of her thumb and forefinger and took the measure of each toe.

"Sarah." He said her name on a groan, a whisper, a sigh.

She slanted a look at him, and the fire in his eyes dazzled her so that she couldn't look away. She wet her dry lips with the tip of her tongue.

"I didn't know feet could be so erotic," she whispered.

"Nor did I."

He was making love to her with his eyes. Even Sarah knew that. Driven by an instinct as old as time, she scooted closer, then cradled his feet on her lap.

Lightning bolts shot through Jim. He could feel the heat of her through the soles of his feet. The heat of promise.

The air around them became somnolent and heavy, inducing a dreamlike state where thoughts are as light as butterflies and hearts as pure as angels.

Sarah closed her eyes and went limp, her head dangling on her slender neck like a flower wilted by too much heat.

Body heat. It burned through him like comets. Sweat beaded his face and dampened his shirt. He sat mesmerized while Sarah's hands drifted lightly over his skin.

Beyond them, near the shoreline a tern called to its mate in plaintive voice and far out over the water a line of brown pelicans floated through the sun-struck sky like tiny boats. Their bit of beach spread with a blanket that harked back to days when buffalo roamed the plains and legends sprang up like flowers, became an island. Jim and Sarah were castaways set adrift in a sea of passion, the only two people in the universe.

The thing that saved him, the thing that saved them both, was honor. Rusty and tarnished but still usable.

Sarah deserved more. It was that simple. Jim had nothing to offer. He was out of work, out of luck and out of heart. The only things he had left were honor and pride.

But how was he to tell a lovely woman with soft lips and gentle hands that he wouldn't make love to her? If he used the wheelchair as an excuse she might protest that his condition didn't matter. He would feel pitied, and she would feel cheated.

He couldn't tell her that he didn't want her. That would be a lie, and she would see right through it.

In battle the wise thing was sometimes not a frontal assault nor even a flanking maneuver, but a diversion.

Jim searched the horizon, then turned to the sea. And there in silver splendor lay his salvation.

"The dolphins are playing in the surf."

Sarah came slowly out of her sensuous stupor. With eyes too bright she broke contact then scooted away from Jim as if he were suddenly a stranger.

"I see them."

Shading her eyes, she turned a flushed face toward the dolphins.

Jim's relief was temporary, then loss settled like a stone over his heart. He put on his socks and shoes while Sarah watched the drama of dolphins unfolding in the sparkling waters.

When she turned back to him, she was all business. Almost. A rosy blush still spread across her cheekbones, and she had the slightly bedazzled look of a woman who has stayed too long on a carousel.

"I brought some more information on my students."

While he read the statistics she gave a thumbnail sketch of her boys, each one heartbreaking.

"You still didn't tell me what I'm supposed to do, Sarah."

"All I want from you is your heart and your soul." Her color deepened, and she wet her lips with the tip of her tongue.

"For my boys," she added.

Quick, relentless desire overtook him once more, and Jim became reckless.

"And for yourself, Sarah? Don't you ever want anything for yourself?"

"Of course, I have dreams. I'm a real flesh and blood person."

"I've noticed."

Jim captured Sarah with a single look, and as he gazed at her he saw the ocean in her eyes, the sun, the entire universe.

*Here is a woman worth knowing.* He thought how little he knew about Sarah. He knew small details of her past from the stories her father had told. He knew the kind impulses that sent her straight into the bear's den with a four-layer chocolate cake. He knew her love for the downtrodden, the underdog.

And he knew her joy of dancing in the garden in the moonlight.

"Tell me your dreams, Sarah."

"I dream of being the kind of teacher who can turn the lives of my students around."

"That's a worthy goal, but I want to know what you dreamed about as a child."

Sarah fiddled with her hair, then leaned over and drew angels in the sand.

"What did you dream about as a child, Jim?"

"Flying. Always flying."

"You made your dreams come true." She slanted him a sideways look. "I didn't. I wanted to be a dancer."

"I've seen you dance in the garden."

She avoided his eyes by turning back to her sand drawings, adding haloes to her angels.

From years of being there for his brother Ben, Jim understood how sometimes waiting in patience reaps far greater rewards than prodding with questions. And so he turned his face up to the sun and waited.

Sarah shifted, and he could tell by the way her body tensed that she was getting ready to bare her soul. He made a vow to himself he would always treat it with tender care.

"Dad and I were living in Boston. I studied dancing with the best teachers in the northeast. I never wanted to be the one on center stage. I knew I didn't have what it takes to be a prima ballerina."

She was quiet for a long time, then she shrugged.

"As it turns out I didn't have what it takes to be a dancer, period." She gave him a bright look, a false smile that he saw as a cover-up. "We keep getting sidetracked. Where were we?"

"We were discussing what you want from me at Southside."

"For one thing, I want you to teach these boys to play basketball. Southside doesn't have money for a coach, but we have one goal without a net. That's a good start. And with your expertise, it will be an excellent start.''

''Don't you want me to scale Mount Everest while I'm at it?''

''You went to college on a basketball scholarship. You could have played pro ball if you hadn't chosen the military.''

Jim was secretly pleased that Sarah knew the details of his life. Through the years, reporters covering the performances of the Blue Angels had dug up and written about almost every aspect of Jim's life, including a secondhand account of the way Bethany had jilted him.

Had Sarah searched the old newspapers *before* she decided to recruit him, or afterward? He'd like to think it was before. He'd like to believe that from the very beginning Sarah Sloan was as intrigued with him as he had been with her.

''I see you did your homework.''

''It wasn't hard. It's all there for anybody who cares to find out.''

*Do you care, Sarah?* The question was on the tip of Jim's tongue, but he bit it back.

''What other Herculean tasks have you planned for me, Sarah?''

''Just *be there* for my boys. Okay, Jim? They need a role model, and I think you're perfect.''

Jim suddenly felt about ten feet tall, even in his wheelchair.

They stayed on the beach talking until the sun began its spectacular descent, then they fell silent, awestruck as luminescent waters swallowed the bright golden orb.

When they reached home, Sarah said, ''Thank you, Jim,'' then offered her hand. To seal the bargain, he guessed. Only it didn't turn out that way. He couldn't let her go. She was soft and trusting and in his eyes, beautiful, and the touch of her hand brought him such pleasure he wanted to sit that way for the rest of the evening. Simply touching her. Merely holding her hand.

She didn't pull away, but lingered, and her heart was right there in her eyes, shining down at him.

"Touching you, Sarah, is like touching the stars."

Her eyes misted over and she squeezed his hand as if she might never let go. They stayed that way for a small eternity, and then Sarah leaned over and kissed him on the lips. Softly. Tenderly.

"Bethany was a fool," she whispered, then hurried from the van as if demons were chasing her.

Sarah didn't go directly to her father's room when she got home, but sat in her garden in the lengthening shadows and replayed the time she'd spent with the Bear. Every beautiful, tender, exquisite moment.

And she knew beyond a shadow of a doubt that she was falling in love.

"I can't," she whispered. "I *must* not."

Her heart hurt so at the thought that she cried out in pain, for she'd discovered another true thing: impossible love will break the heart in two.

Sarah left the garden slowly and walked carefully up the stairs, holding on to a heart already cracked beyond repair.

Her father and his sitter were waiting for her.

When he got home Jim found the robe she'd borrowed. It had touched Sarah's body intimately, and her scent was caught in its fiber, mingled with his.

He slipped it on, letting the soft folds that had caressed her skin touch his. Then he took the elevator to his rooftop and sat with his head tilted back, gazing up at the stars.

Once he'd owned the heavens. But they were closed to him, now.

Or were they? When he touched Sarah, he felt as if he touched the stars. And when he'd held her in his arms, hadn't he held heaven?

He thought about Sarah and his brother Ben. Both of them wanted him to be a hero. A man who had lost his wings. A man in a wheelchair.

Jim thought of another man in a wheelchair, the actor whose fall from a horse had made him a quadriplegic, the actor who used his name and his celebrity status to bring a message of hope to others like him. Not only to others like him but to every life he touched.

Jim left the rooftop, dressed in sweats and went into his exercise room. The parallel bars gleamed at him through the darkness.

Jim didn't even turn on the light. His wheelchair whirred as he crossed the room. Grasping the bars he pulled himself upright, then held on for dear life, his arms corded, his breathing ragged.

His brother's voice echoed through his mind. "You can do it, Jim. Nothing is keeping you from walking except yourself."

Slowly, ever so slowly he let go—and toppled like a redwood tree.

With his face on the floor, Jim Standing Bear asked the Great Spirit to make him worthy of Sarah's trust, to make him worthy of being Sioux.

## Chapter Seven

"I want you to know we're glad to have you on board at Southside." Dr. Mac Thompson's handshake was firm, his expression sincere.

Jim checked for pity and didn't see any. He began to relax.

"Sarah can be very persuasive."

"So I see." Mac Thompson smiled. "Thank you for coming, Jim."

"Don't thank me yet. I still have to prove myself to Sarah."

Laughing heartily, Mac Thompson directed Jim to her room.

She was sitting in the middle of the floor surrounded by teenage boys nearly twice her size. Even if Jim hadn't read the file, he would have known immediately that Sarah's students were not the typical all-American teens. These boys looked as if they'd gone out of their way to defy all norms of dress and social conduct.

There were two Mohawk haircuts, dyed punk green; one had a shaved head, the baldpate plastered with stick-on tattoos, and three had Afros as big as basketballs. Their dress ranged from Army fatigues with combat boots to jeans so ripped and torn it was hard to see how they managed to stay together. Small gold hoops hung from holes in their ears, their noses, and only God knew what other body parts.

The only thing these ten boys had in common was the look on their faces—a defiant, watchful look that said, even if you show me I don't believe a word you're saying.

Jim sat in the doorway, watching Sarah unaware. The animation on her face transformed her. And transfixed Jim. Even across the room he could feel the force of her passion.

Sarah Sloan loved teaching. That much was clear. From his secluded spot in the hallway he witnessed the same intensity he'd felt when he kissed her.

Watching her, he knew that the real danger in coming to Southside was not in exposing himself to the pity and perhaps the ridicule of strangers, but in exposing himself to the fatal charms of a woman named Sarah Sloan.

Sarah didn't know what had alerted her first—a sound, a movement, a heartbeat gone wild. Suddenly the Bear was there in her doorway, and rainbows shed their brilliance on her small world.

"Come in, Jim. I want you to meet my boys."

Jim Standing Bear was a commanding presence, even in his wheelchair. Counting on the element of surprise, she hadn't given her students any advance warning and it paid off.

"Students, I want you to meet Lieutenant Commander Jim Standing Bear of the Blue Angels."

Her misfit adolescents watched him with equal parts awe and suspicion. Jim sat in his wheelchair enduring their inspection with quiet dignity.

Sampson was the first to break the silence.

"Hey, that's cool man. What kind of plane do you fly?"

"I used to fly an F/A-18 Hornet."

The other boys followed suit, bombarding Jim with questions. All except Archie, her wounded child with his neon-green Mohawk and a father who hated him.

"Big deal," he muttered, then withdrew to a sullen silence at the back of the room.

Sarah didn't press the matter. Instead she moved to her desk and watched a small miracle unfolding with Jim and her other needy boys.

From the back of the room came the slap of a basketball against brick. Over and over Archie heaved the ball. Harder and harder until he was having to jump into the air to catch it as it ricocheted off the wall.

Sarah didn't intervene. The only damage to the old brick wall would be a few places where the paint had chipped. The damage Archie had suffered was much more severe and wouldn't be repaired in a day.

A buzzer sounded for the physical education period.

"Go on outside, boys. I'll meet you there shortly."

After they had gone, she turned to Jim.

"So, what do you think?"

"I think you're expecting miracles."

"Maybe I am. Maybe I'm naive. It would be simple to come here every day and teach these boys reading and math and science, then go home and forget about them. But I want more, Jim. I want to give them hope and dreams. I want to give them a future.''

''I hope they know how lucky they are.''

The way Jim was looking at her made Sarah almost forget about ten rowdy and defiant teenagers rampaging over the playground unsupervised.

''Thank you.''

She leaned down to hug him and was dangerously close to kissing him when Mohammed burst into the room.

''Miss Sloan, you gotta come quick. Archie and Jared are fighting and Archie's got a knife.''

*He's got a knife.* The words ricocheted through Jim like bullets.

Sarah was headed toward the door, straight into the arms of danger.

''Sarah, wait,'' he called, but it was too late.

She was already out the door, her footsteps hammering down the hallway.

''Get Dr. Thompson,'' she yelled.

Jim looked at Mohammed. ''Do it,'' he commanded, then he was chasing Sarah, silently cursing the damnable slowness of his wheelchair while a thousand nightmares played through his mind.

Sarah trapped between two angry young men who had learned to fight dirty in mean streets and dark alleys. Sarah with the blade of a knife at her throat. Sarah white and fallen, her neck blooming like a rose.

Fear turned his blood to ice. His wheelchair bumped over the threshold and onto the campus. And there was Sarah, standing on the edge of a tight little circle around the fighters—Jared in a boxing stance and Archie with a knife.

Jim knew he could disarm the boy, even in a wheel-chair.

"Sarah, stand back," he yelled.

"Archie, give me the knife."

Apparently, she hadn't heard. Jim worked furiously at the controls of his wheelchair, seeking an added burst of speed that wasn't there.

"Back off, teacher," Archie shouted, glaring at her.

Fear for her formed a tight knot in Jim's stomach.

"Sarah! Do as he says."

She swung her head in his direction and he could see the fear and confusion on her face.

"Do it, Sarah!"

He followed his order with a look that had caused grown men to cringe. Slowly Sarah swiveled back to the boys, *her* boys.

"Archie, please, *please* think about what you're do-ing. Don't do anything you're going to regret for the rest of your life."

Her plea only exacerbated Archie's anger.

"Shut up!" Archie yelled. "Shut the hell up!"

Jim had seen situations like this before. He'd seen how otherwise sane and sensible men could snap when equal parts rage and fear worked through them.

The wheelchair moved with glacial slowness. The boys were still squared off, Archie with the knife poised and Jared with sweat pouring down his face.

The other boys, sensing something too strong, too dangerous to view up close, moved back, further ex-posing Sarah to Archie's fury.

Sometimes a display of superior strength could dif-fuse the situation.

"Archie! Drop the knife!" Jim commanded, hoping

he was right in this case. Tension was so thick it had a smell.

"Who are you telling what to do, cripple?"

"You. Drop the weapon."

"Stay back, old man," Archie shouted, but he was beginning to waver. "You'll only get in the way."

Some of the rage had drained out of him. Jim could tell by the loosening of his body, the slight tremble in his hands.

Sarah saw it, too.

"You don't want to do this," she said softly.

Then she started moving toward the boy, and in that instant everything changed. Archie snaked out one arm and grabbed Sarah.

If he lived to be a hundred, Jim would never forget her scream. It cut through him like a knife.

Jim was up and running, the wheelchair overturned in the dirt, his legs pumping as if they'd never forgotten how to run, his battle cry pure savage Sioux.

Years of hand-to-hand combat training came into play. He captured Archie in one swift move, twisting the arm that held the weapon. The knife fell to the ground and lay in the dirt like an obscenity.

The crowd stood dumbfounded. Sarah's hand flew to her mouth, and she made a sound like a baby bird fallen from its safe, familiar nest.

"It's all right, Sarah," Jim said, his voice calm. "Everything's all right."

And suddenly it was. Fear for Sarah had catapulted Jim out of his wheeled prison, and he was standing on his own two legs with his feet planted on the ground for the first time since his accident. Planted *firmly*.

There was no swaying. No weakness in the knees.

No certainty that within the next few minutes his face would kiss the ground.

Jim Standing Bear was reclaiming his identity. He was reclaiming his life.

"Jim, you walked," Sarah whispered, and in her eyes shone the knowledge that he had done it for her.

## *Chapter Eight*

Jim was in the shabbiest part of town standing in front of a tenement house that looked as if it should be condemned. The only way he could explain his presence there was Sarah.

The look on her face when the principal had suspended Archie for carrying a weapon onto the school grounds had ripped Jim's heart in two.

After the principal left she'd turned to him in soft and lovely supplication.

"Oh, Jim. Can't we do something?"

"The rules are good ones, Sarah. We can't change them."

What he could change, though, was the sadness on Sarah's face.

He hoped. And prayed.

After what had happened on campus that day, Jim

knew beyond a shadow of a doubt that his hot line was open with the Father Creator.

Sending a prayer winging upward, he walked up the rotting steps and knocked on the door. A woman with twigs of hair wrapped in foil stuck her head out the window. The sun glinting on her head made her look like a creature from outer space.

"Whadda ya want?" she yelled.

"I'm looking for Archie," Jim said, and within minutes the boy was walking toward him with a lifetime of anger coiled tightly in his belly and defeat stamped on his face.

Now there was no turning back.


The excitement of the day was still on Sarah when she got home, and she poured out the story to her sister.

"You should have seen him, Julie," she said after she'd recounted Jim's heroics on the campus of Southside. "He was magnificent."

Julie gathered her scarf and purse before replying. Sarah knew what that meant. She was in for one of Julie's *big sister* lectures.

"Let me get this straight. Jim Standing Bear walked, just like one of those miracles you see on TV evangelistic shows, and you don't say it was exciting or even miraculous. Instead you tell me that *he* was *magnificent.*"

"If you had been there, you'd have said the same thing."

"I see." Julie pursed her lips and gave her famous look.

Sarah knew what that meant, too. Lord knows, she should. She'd seen it enough while they were growing up. The *look* meant that Julie was not only going to lecture, she was going to try and take charge.

She tried to forestall Julie's avalanche of advice by retreat.

"Forget it."

"Forget it! You want me to forget that you've spent the last fifteen minutes extolling the virtues of Jim Standing Bear, who, might I add, is perhaps the most delicious-looking man I've seen since college."

Sarah's blush gave her away, and she silently raged at the fates for giving her such a telltale signal. Wasn't it enough that her face was plain? Did it have to be as readable as a billboard, too?

"It's not like that, Julie."

"Why not, Sarah?"

"You know the answer to that as well as I do. I'm not exactly Queen of the May, and besides that, I have responsibilities."

"He's my father, too, Sarah. Or have you forgotten that?"

"No, it's just that you have a family to take care of and I don't. Except Dad. He's my primary concern, Julie."

"I'll declare, Sarah, for someone so smart you are about the most dense person I've ever known. Sometimes I just want to wring your neck."

"How did the sitter do today?"

"Okay, and don't change the subject. When are you going to quit hiding and start *living,* Sarah? That's what I want to know."

The truth hit Sarah with a staggering force. Since she'd moved next door to Jim Standing Bear she'd tasted life. And it was delicious.

She glanced out the window and across to the rooftop where she'd first seen him, her Blue Angel.

"Sarah?" Julie put a hand on her shoulder. "I want only the best for you because you're my sister and I love you."

"Tomorrow, Julie."

"Tomorrow, what?"

"That's when I'm going to start living."

For the first time since she'd been teaching, Sarah became a clock-watcher. Fifteen more minutes and the bell would ring. Fifteen more minutes and she could see Jim. After all, he'd saved her life yesterday and she hadn't even thanked him properly.

She'd planned to do that yesterday but after Julie left, her dad and the sitter got into an argument and Sarah rushed upstairs to make the peace.

"He wants me to dance," the sitter had told her, and the look on Evelyn Grimes's face told Sarah exactly what she thought of that notion. "I wasn't hired to dance."

"Ginger's gone and I need a new dance partner."

Her father was wearing the top hat he'd found at the flea market in Searsport, Maine, years ago when he and Sarah had gone up to visit one of her college friends who lived in a cottage on Penobscot Bay. At the time he'd been pleased to find something that reminded him of the great old veterans of dance he so admired, Gene Kelly and Fred Astaire, and now it had become his identity.

He two-stepped around his sitter, then swept off his hat and bowed from the waist.

"They're playing our song, Cyd."

"Who's Cyd?"

"Cyd Charisse," Sarah said. "A great dancer." Sarah took her father's hand. "Hello, Fred. I'm back."

"Ginger?"

"Yes, it's Ginger."

"You've been gone a long time."

"I know, but I'm back now and I want to dance. Will you dance with me?"

"My pleasure."

Her father swept off his top hat and bent over Sarah's hand. Then he swung her into a slow stately waltz. Sarah could almost hear the strains of the "Blue Danube."

The school bell cut into Sarah's thoughts. With anticipation singing through her blood like new wine, she dismissed her class and hurried home.

Julie met her at the door. "Have you been in your garden?"

"Seeing my garden is the last thing on my mind today."

Sarah tossed her books onto the hall table and wondered whether she should take the time to put on lipstick.

"I think you should take a look."

"I'm in a hurry, Julie. The garden will have to wait."

"Go to your garden, Sarah. I insist."

"Good grief. I have things to do, important things. What is all this silly business about the garden?"

Julie caught her shoulders and turned her toward the door.

"Just go out there and look. You'll find out for yourself."

Sarah was set to argue, but her sister waved her outside.

"Go on. Scat. Shoo. Dad's asleep and the sitter's having tea in the kitchen and I'm headed home to see what my hellions did in school today."

"All right, Julie. You win. Is it all right if I get my garden hat first?"

"Whatever." Julie was grinning like a cat that had swallowed the canary.

Sarah felt grumpy when she went out the door. She was anxious to go through the hedge and see Jim. Why had she let her sister talk her into going to the garden?

The answer was simple. She could never stand firm in the face of Julie's persuasions.

Maybe she ought to take her hoe. Maybe Julie had discovered an exotic type of weed growing out there. That was ridiculous, of course. Julie didn't know a weed from a petunia.

Still out of sorts, Sarah pushed open the garden gate.

"Surprise, Sarah."

Jim was standing in the middle of a garden paradise. Azaleas and forsythias and hawthorne competed for attention with hyacinths and jonquils and tulips. And in the midst of it all stood a star magnolia dripping with white blossoms.

Her ruined garden had been transformed. It was spectacular. But more spectacular still was the sight of Jim *walking*. She still couldn't get over the miracle of it.

"Do you like your garden, Sarah?"

"Like it? I *love* it."

"I'm glad."

"*You* did this?"

"I'd love to take full credit, but I can't. Actually I had a little help from Archie."

"Archie?" Sarah was so dumbfounded she could

hardly speak. "How did that happen? What's going on?"

"Come." He caught her hand and led her to the garden bench. "Sit beside me and I'll tell you all about it."

She sat on a stone bench in the shade of an ancient chinaberry tree beside the fountain and took off her hat. When Jim sat beside her close enough so that their thighs touched, she felt feminine and desirable, exciting, even. She felt like a woman full of mysteries and possibilities.

Sarah could have stayed that way forever. Caught up in the wonder of the moment, she became purely selfish. She didn't want to hear news about her garden, her students, or even her father.

"In the short time I've known you, Sarah, I've seen your love of two things—your students and your garden."

"I used to watch you watching me from the rooftop," she murmured.

"I wanted to make the garden beautiful for you, Sarah."

"No man except my father has ever wanted to make anything beautiful for me. I'm overwhelmed," she said, her eyes misting.

"Tears?"

"I always cry when I'm happy."

She could no more stop the tears that trickled down her cheeks than she could stop the sun from rising in the east. Jim wiped them away with such tenderness, Sarah cried all the harder.

"You must *really* be happy, Sarah."

How could she possibly explain to him the true nature of her tears? How could she tell a man who was so gorgeous he'd probably had women falling at his feet all his life that she had never felt the tenderness of any man? Except her father, of course, and that didn't count.

It was romance that Sarah longed for. Romance that she'd prayed for as she stood on the sidelines and watched men pay homage to her sister's beauty and charm.

No man had even found Sarah charming. She considered that a particularly painful failure since her father had spared no expense to provide his daughters with schooling in every social grace known to man.

The schooling didn't take on Sarah. At least that's what she had thought. Until today. Until a dark warrior named Bear had come into her garden and made her feel worthy of paradise.

His hands were still on her face, and she hardly breathed for fear he would take them away. Yesterday she'd told her sister that she was going to start living, *really* living.

Her blood sang like a chorus of birds celebrating the first flowers of spring. Her skin flamed as if somebody had lit torches underneath. Her mouth was dry.

And she didn't want it to end. Not for a long, long while.

But how was she going to keep him interested? What was the next step? She wished she'd spent more time reading romance novels and less reading textbooks.

What good was the latest education theory when your heart was on fire?

Jim's eyes burned through her. His fingers caressed her cheeks.

"Sarah, the sight of your happiness moves me to tears."

He was telling the truth. His dark eyes were suspiciously bright and a bit of moisture was caught on his eyelashes. Were all men so honest about their emotions?

Sarah hadn't a clue. Why should she? The only man she'd known up close was this Sioux warrior who was exceptional in every way. She couldn't possibly use him as a measure of ordinary men. He was not merely head and shoulders above; he was mountains above. He was Everest while every other man was a modest knoll in the foothills of the Appalachians.

Jim leaned toward Sarah, his intent stamped clearly on his face. He was going to kiss her.

Had Julie left? Sarah thought so. She vaguely remembered hearing the sound of a car soon after she opened the garden gate.

Then there was Jim, and nothing else had mattered.

His lips brushed hers softly, and she closed her eyes, forgetting to breathe. The heavens were wrapped up in his kiss, and through it all she smelled the fragrance of flowers.

His touch was fleeting, his kiss brief, but in it she had seen how tenderness can be one of the most important elements in a relationship.

Jim shifted so that they were no longer touching, and a bit self-consciously he stared out across the garden. But Sarah was content. Sitting beside him in quiet companionship filled her with contentment.

A cardinal flew down and perched in the empty birdbath, pecking at bits of seed that had landed there, wind-borne. Robins, fat with the bounty the earth provided every spring, scratched the newly turned flower beds. And high on the ancient brick wall a mocking-bird scolded them all.

"Tell me about Archie, Jim."

"He's working for me while he's on probation, and I'm tutoring him so he won't fall so far behind."

Without fanfare, Jim had handed Sarah another miracle.

"I was worried sick about him," she said.

"I know. That's why I'm helping him."

"For me?"

"All for you." He laughed. "But don't think I do this kind of thing every day. I'm basically a very selfish man, Sarah."

"Oh, I can see that. I've never seen a more selfish creature in all my life."

She leaned over and kissed his cheek. "You don't fool me for a minute, Jim Standing Bear. I've known since the first day I met you that you're a kind man."

"In view of my behavior, I don't know how you determined that."

"Delta told me."

Jim exploded with laughter. "And what else did the Mouth of the South tell you about me?"

"Oh, terrible things. That you turn down the pages of books instead of using a bookmark, that you use too much butter on your popcorn, and that you have never once in all the years she's known you eaten an oyster."

Sarah stopped, breathless and surprised. She'd never known how to make small talk. Why was it so easy with Jim? Would *everything* be that easy with him?

Her thoughts took a naughty turn, and she blushed the color of the azaleas.

Jim studied her for a long time, and she blushed even darker.

"Care to share that thought with me, Sarah?"

"I don't think so."

"You're a woman of secrets, are you?"

With one statement he'd made her sound intriguing instead of shy and awkward. Her heart flowered like a camellia, and all the love songs she'd ever danced to poured through her mind.

Why had she ever thought those phrases were trite? In her garden where miracles happened, Sarah knew that some of the most absolute truths were contained in the lyrics of Broadway show tunes.

The sun began its western descent, and the garden was filled with soft purple shadows and the dying glow of gold. Jim stood.

Sarah felt like a child suddenly deprived of her favorite candy.

"You're leaving?"

"For now." Bending down, he kissed her hand in a grand gesture worthy of nineteenth-century Southern gentlemen. "I'll come back, Sarah. And when I do, I'm going to discover all your secrets."

Sarah sat on her garden bench hugging his delicious promise to herself. She didn't go inside until the sitter called to her from the front porch.

And then she didn't walk. She floated.


Jim was whistling when he went inside. Courting Sarah Sloan was going to be fun.

*And then what?* The question nagged at him while he heated a bowl of chicken and dumplings Delta had made. Resolutely, he shoved the worrisome question from his mind.

He had just started walking again. Didn't he deserve to enjoy himself for a while? Sarah made him feel alive. She made him feel good about himself and about life in general.

And for right now, that was enough. His future was still murky, his plans uncertain. Sarah was the only concrete thing in his life, the only certainty.

He wanted her, and if he wasn't mistaken, she wanted him. What could be simpler?

## Chapter Nine

"You knew he was in the garden all along."

Julie laughed so hard, Sarah had to hold the telephone away from her ear.

"Of course I knew. He came to the door with that sullen young man and asked my permission to plant your garden. Are you complaining, Sarah?"

"No, not at all. It was a nice surprise."

"Nice? That's not exactly the word I'd use to describe Jim Standing Bear."

"It was *wonderful*, Julie. The most wonderful thing that has ever happened to me." Sarah twisted the phone cord around her fingers. "I think he's going to ask me out. I can't be sure, but it sounded that way."

"Of course he's going to ask you out. Why shouldn't he?"

"I could give you about a dozen good reasons, starting with this dress I'm wearing."

"I'm going to take you shopping and we're going to get you a whole new wardrobe, something suitable for the exotic, exciting woman you are."

"There's no need to go overboard, Julie. A small white lie will do. Anyhow, new clothes are moot. I can't go out with Jim Standing Bear."

"Why not, I'd like to know?"

"I mean, he might not ask me out, anyhow, but if he does, who would watch after Dad?"

"The night sitter."

"We don't have a night sitter."

"We're going to hire one. I've been meaning to, anyhow. You can't teach school if you keep losing sleep over Dad's night prowlings."

What Julie said was true. Last week he'd awakened Sarah three nights in a row dancing in the hallway with his top hat and cane and wearing his nightshirt. And just last night she'd caught him at three o'clock in the morning fully dressed and trying to open the dead bolt locks to the front door.

Sarah had taken to sleeping with the key.

"I suppose you're right, Julie."

"I know I'm right."

"Why don't we ask Mrs. Grimes to take the night shift and get somebody else for the daytime? I don't think he's happy with her."

"Who would be? I think if she ever smiled her face would fall off. Tomorrow why don't you ask Delta if she knows somebody to take the day shift? Somebody happy."

By the time Sarah got up on Saturday morning, Delta was already in the sunroom, eradicating dust and singing a low-country ballad.

"Delta, do you know anybody who would be a good sitter for the day shift with Dad?"

"You gettin' rid of that ole sourpuss?"

"We're moving her to the night shift."

"Hallelujah. It's like a funeral home around with her. My sister's looking for a job, and she wouldn't be all the time pussyfooting around here looking like a prune, neither."

"If she's just like you, I'll hire her sight unseen."

"That depends on what you mean."

"Is she a cross between the Rock of Gibraltar and a carousel?"

"That's Savannah to a tee."

"I have one other question. Does she dance?"

"She was born dancing."

"She's hired."

Within an hour the new plan was in place, and Sarah took her breakfast out to the garden. The sight of the flowers moved her to tears.

Jim Standing Bear had created all this beauty for her. Only for her. Her heart set up such a clamor, she put her hand over her chest to calm it down.

"Don't make too much of this," she whispered.

Her mind took note, but her heart just kept up its runaway rhythm.

"Sarah," Delta called from the front porch. "Telephone." She grinned from ear to ear. "It's Jim."

The mistake Jim had made with Bethany was in doing all the things she loved and none of the things he enjoyed. As a result he'd fallen for a woman whose only interest in him turned out to be his celebrity status.

He wasn't going to make the same mistake twice.

He was going to find out right off the bat if he and Sarah had anything in common except passion.

Not that he was planning to fall for Sarah Sloan. Not by a long shot. She was a sweet and lovely woman, absolutely desirable and totally irresistible.

And she deserved somebody who could give her the moon.

All Jim could give her was a star or two. Starting today.

He rang her bell, and she was smiling when she came to the door. She was also swathed in enough clothes to see an Eskimo through an ice storm—a big sun hat, sunglasses, a long-sleeved shirt, long pants. Was that a bathing suit strap he glimpsed? He hoped so.

"I take it you don't like sun," he said.

"Only in small doses."

"Ever fished?"

"No."

Jim's hopes fell. "Maybe this isn't such a good idea, then. Would you rather go somewhere else? The art gallery? A movie?"

Her laughter was as clear and soul-soothing as silver bells in clear mountain air.

"Goodness, no." He loved the way she caught her lower lip between her teeth when she looked at him. "Unless you would."

"Let's go fishing, Sarah."

His boat was an old cabin cruiser he kept in top-notch condition. It was stocked with everything a serious fisherman needed. Bethany had refused to set foot on it. She'd said it smelled of fish.

As he helped Sarah onto the boat he watched her with the critical eye of a protective parent seeing whether his only child will be accepted on the first day of school.

"Oh, my," she said.

Was that good or bad? Jim was afraid to ask.

"Is this real teakwood?"

"Yes. This is an old boat. They don't make them like this anymore. They use fiberglass now."

Sarah ran her hands over the satiny surface, worn smooth from years of sun and wind and rain.

"It's absolutely beautiful."

Jim was smiling when he took the wheel. So far, so good.

"Hang on to your hat, Sarah. We're taking her out into deeper water."

Sarah was already in deeper water, and had been the minute she'd said *yes* to Jim's invitation to fish. With the wind in his hair and the sun on his face he looked like a bronzed god. Thank goodness her hands were occupied holding on to her hat. Otherwise she'd have been doing something completely foolish, like running them through his dark hair and over his broad chest.

"Look, Sarah. Brown pelicans."

She turned her head in the direction he pointed, and her hat sailed into the water and headed out to sea. Jim cut the motor.

"Don't worry, Sarah. I'll try to get it."

"You'd do that for me?"

"Absolutely." He was already stripping off his shirt. The sight of his bare chest almost made her swoon.

"Please, no." She put a hand on his arm. "I've

discovered I like the wind in my hair and the sun on my face.''

''Such a lovely face.''

His fingers trailed lightly over her cheeks, and she thought she'd died and gone to heaven. The two of them were alone in the boat in the middle of the bay. They might as well have been the only two people in the world. It felt that isolated. And that wonderful.

''I don't want you to burn,'' he said. ''Let me get the sunblock.''

Jim disappeared into the small cabin. All Sarah could see was the bottom half of him. And it was just as gorgeous as the top.

''Oh, help,'' she whispered. Why hadn't Julie given her some good advice instead of the ridiculously tiny bikini she wore under her clothes?

''It's not as big as a handkerchief,'' Sarah had told her sister.

''That's the general idea.''

Jim reappeared with the sunscreen. ''Come here, Sarah.''

The command was soft and seductive, and she went to him like a woman sleepwalking. Smiling down into her eyes, he began to rub the lotion on her face. It took every ounce of her self-control to keep from moaning.

''I can do that,'' she protested, but not very vigorously. After all, how vigorous could a stick of melted butter be?

''You might miss a spot.'' His hands were on her neck now, massaging the tiny V of skin visible above her shirt. ''I wouldn't want one inch of that soft skin burned.''

Sarah closed her eyes and gave herself up to pleasure.

"You like that, don't you, Sarah?"

Oh, God, he was making love to her with his voice. Sarah's knees were so weak she could barely stand.

"Umm," she murmured. "Very much. I think I'm becoming a hedonist."

"My favorite kind of person."

His hands were on the back of her neck now, doing things far more significant than spreading sunscreen. Sarah, a hedonist newly born, began to unbutton her shirt. For once in her life she didn't think about responsibility and propriety. She didn't think about being plain.

All she knew was that the moment was glorious and golden, and so was the man. All she knew was that his hands were caressing her face and neck and she wanted them all over her. Now. This very minute. While opportunity thundered at her door.

After all, men like Jim Standing Bear came along only once in a lifetime.

"Would you do my back, too?"

The blouse slid from her shoulders and she heard his sharp intake of breath. Sarah opened her eyes, for suddenly she didn't want to miss a single thing.

Jim was looking at her as if he'd discovered treasures beyond compare. Or maybe that's what she wanted to see. Maybe he looked at all women with a hungry gleam in his eye.

"Such perfection should only be viewed by the gods," he said, and then his hands were on her shoulders, moving inward along her collarbone.

As if to compensate for her face, God had given her

a body that rounded in all the right places, and for that she was eternally grateful. So it seemed, was Jim.

His hands played lightly over the tops of her breasts, spreading the cream in slow dreamy movements. Sarah stood proud and tall, electrocuted by desire.

"Why don't we go down below?" he said.

Sarah would have followed him to the moon. Going down a small flight of steps was going to be no effort at all.

"Yes," she whispered. "Oh, yes."

Jim couldn't believe what was happening. Passion had ambushed him. Desire held him captive.

He hadn't meant it to be this way. He'd planned to show Sarah how to fish, to cook the catch over some nice hot coals on the beach, and then to seduce her slowly while the moon rode like a galleon in a night filled with stars. In short, he'd planned an evening of romance.

Was it the sight of that wisp of red satin around her lush breasts that had set him off like a rocket, or had he gone into orbit the minute his hands touched her face?

"It's close in here. Watch your step."

He was the one watching her. Somewhere between the top step and the bottom she'd shed her slacks, and now she stood before him a vision in red with a body that would make grown men weep. Her legs were long and slender, beautifully toned. All that dancing, he guessed.

He pulled her slowly into his arms, and she gazed at him with the wide-eyed, flushed look of an innocent. It was a beautiful illusion that set his blood on fire. Whether he would admit it or not, every man dreams of being the first for a woman. Every man longs to believe that he's the only one who has ever touched her, ever made her feel sexual hunger, ever shown her the indescribable joy of making love.

In this day and age they were pipe dreams, of course, but there in the tight confines of that cabin with the boat rocking gently on the sun-struck waters, Jim Standing Bear saw himself as that kind of hero. Sarah did that to a man.

And perhaps that was her greatest charm.

Perhaps that was why he was struggling so with control.

Jim liked his loving slow and leisurely. He liked to savor a woman, to take his time with the seduction, to stand back, both emotionally and physically, and watch passion build until she was humming like the strings of a guitar drawn too tight.

Sarah shattered all his long-held notions. With her, he was savage, a ravening beast who stripped aside her miniscule top and closed his mouth greedily over her breasts. Feasting. Exulting. Glorying in the sweet soft mounds of fragrant flesh and the electrifying response of her body.

Shivers shook her, and the nipples that were already responsive hardened to diamond points. Jim's tongue toyed, teased, bathed, and when that was not enough, he took her deep into his mouth, groaning with a pleasure that shook him all the way to his toes.

A red light went on in his brain. *Caution,* it signaled. *This woman is different.*

The warning was far too late. Jim was already over the brink. Sarah was under his skin so deep she'd burrowed somewhere in the vicinity of his soul. If he didn't have her, he would die.

It was that simple.

Her hands wove into his hair, and she pulled him closer, arching her back and offering herself up to him like the goddess she was.

"I can't get enough of you," he murmured, and she made a small unintelligible sound, half moan, half plea.

His hands skimmed over her body, memorizing, discovering. Hooking his thumbs in her waistband, he stripped her of the remaining bit of cloth, then picked her up and carried her to his bed.

"Watch your head," he said. "It's going to be a tight fit."

She blushed even deeper, and he was thrilled. She laughed, a low, throaty seductive sound that filled the tiny cabin, and he was hooked.

"I've never known anyone like you, Sarah."

She wrapped her arms around him and pulled him closer. "Don't talk, Jim, just love me." She rained kisses around his mouth and on his throat, and by the time she got to his chest Jim Standing Bear didn't know whether he was coming or going, as his flying buddy Ace Jones of Arkansas often said.

This was the first time Jim had ever found the saying apt.

A small shaft of light poured through the narrow doorway, and he laid Sarah in the golden pathway that fell across the bed. She was luminous. Whether it was her silky skin that had been shielded from the burning rays of the sun or whether it was a trick of light, Jim couldn't say. All he knew was that he wanted her more than he'd ever wanted another woman.

Bending over her he kissed the indention at the base of her throat. She smelled of sunshine, sunscreen and roses. Jim wanted to take her in through his very pores.

He inhaled her, tasted her, savored her. To Jim's delight she gave herself completely over to pleasure. She moaned and purred and arched.

He traced an erotic path across her turgid nipples, under the soft scented mounds then downward to the tiny indention of her navel.

"I never dreamed..."

Her voice trailed away on a soft sigh, and she shivered as he continued his delicious exploration.

"Relax, Sarah," he whispered. "Go with it."

With gentle pressure he parted her legs and found the sweet hot core of her passion. And when he dipped his fingers inside, her body arched upward like a fish.

He'd never known a woman so sensitive to touch. And it drove him wild. His fingers plyed deeper, and she cried out as if she'd been gut-punched.

She tangled her fingers in his hair, alternately pulling him closer and pushing him back.

"I think I'm dying," she said, the words spaced between deep gasps and excited moanings.

Her reaction goaded Jim, ignited him. He was stallion and she was spurs. He was flame and she was oxygen.

Need ripped through him like a tornado, tearing away the last shred of his control. Poised above her, Jim memorized every single detail—the way her hair fanned out on his pillows, the way the sun seemed caught in the center of her green eyes, the way she worried her full lower lip between her teeth.

Wanting to savor every minute, he entered her slowly. Sarah sucked in a sharp breath. Jim moved deeper and met a sweet tight barrier.

His heart thundered like war drums. Sarah trembled beneath him, her body bowed upward, her eyes so luminous he could see straight through to her soul.

"Sarah?"

Wonder filled Jim, and on its heels regret. He had taken her carelessly to his bed without thought of anything except pleasure, and in the process he'd almost deflowered a virgin.

Not just any virgin, but Sarah Sloan, a sweet giving woman who became Ginger Rogers in her garden because her father thought he was Fred Astaire, a generous woman whose heart was big enough for every wounded child she saw, a rather shy woman who had taken the shreds of a dream and woven them into a lifetime career of service to others.

"Why didn't you tell me?"

He started to withdraw, but she clutched him tightly, held on to him as if she meant never to let go.

"I thought you wouldn't want me."

"My God. I've wanted you from the first time I ever saw you."

A shudder shook her, and tears spilled down her cheeks. Jim withdrew, then pulled her close and buried his face in her hair.

"I'm sorry, Sarah," he whispered. "I'm so sorry."

"Oh, please, please don't say that." She pressed her face into his shoulder, and her tears burned him like branding irons.

He thought she was crying for innocence lost. While her virginity was still intact, he'd taken the intimate liberties of a bridegroom, and forever robbed her of some of the joy of discovery on her wedding day.

As old-fashioned and impossible as it seemed, Sarah Sloan was a vanishing breed, a truly innocent woman who had probably been saving herself for the marriage bed. He'd almost stolen that from her. Nothing he could do, nothing he could say would make up for what he had done.

"If I had known, Sarah. If only I had known..."

"If you had known, would you have brought me down here?"

"No."

The silence that filled the room was heavy with regret, eloquent with unspoken pleadings. Then suddenly Sarah's tears vanished and her trembling ceased. Slowly she wound her arms around him and moved her hips with a natural eroticism that had Jim groaning.

"Sarah. Don't." he pulled his hips back, hoping that small separation would be enough.

It wasn't. Passion stormed through him, almost ripping aside his control.

"You don't know what you're doing," he said.

"I do." She snuggled into him once more, her body supple and sweat-slick, her eyes wide and pleading. "Make love to me, Jim."

"It would be so easy, Sarah." He smoothed her damp hair back and kissed her forehead. "So very easy."

"*Please,* Jim."

"Don't ask that of me, Sarah."

Her lower lip trembled, and she took a deep breath, fighting for control. How could he tell her no without hurting her feelings? And yet, how could he do what she asked without destroying her future?

Women like Sarah Sloan needed promises and commitment and vows. Jim Standing Bear was in no position to be making promises.

"Both of us are caught up right now in the heat of passion, Sarah. I'm not going to do something you will regret tomorrow."

"I won't regret it."

"*I* would. Not that I made love to you, but that I stole something precious, something that can never be replaced."

"I feel so...so *incomplete*. You've awakened feelings in me I've never known. I want...I need." Her lips trembled and her eyes grew moist. "Oh, Jim...*please*."

She was impossible to resist. And so Jim struck a compromise between his honor and her need.

He kissed her tenderly then gathered her close and whispered against her fragrant hair, "I can give you some release."

"Yes...please."

"And still leave you..."

"Shh. Don't say it, Jim." She wove her fingers through his hair and pulled him down to her breasts. "Show me."

His mouth closed over her breast, and she became sensitized and electric, trembling with his touch. Pulling her nipple deep into his mouth, Jim began to suckle. Sarah writhed, calling out his name in whispered sighs and soft moanings.

"Jim...I want...I need... *Please*."

Never leaving her breast, Jim ran his hand down the smooth planes of her belly. And when his fingers slid inside, Sarah arched upward, keening with pleasure.

Jim had done this before, many times. He knew the secret places, understood how to make the magic happen. What he hadn't known was that this time the magic would happen to him.

Plying her sweet depths with tenderness and passion and wonder, he lifted his head to look at Sarah.

Discovery transformed her.

Her breathing quickened, her eyes widened, her body loosened. She flowed under him like silk. She burned through him like flame. She invaded him like a Sioux war party.

He became her captive. Her master. Her teacher. Her pupil.

"Oh," she cried. "I never knew. I never knew."

She was shining, joyful, and Jim wished he could give her the moon.

All he could give her was a sweet, tender release.

"This is only the beginning, Sarah."

He caught her hands and wove her fingers tightly through his. Her palms were damp and a fine sheen of perspiration lay upon her skin.

Bending down he licked her dew-kissed lips, then claimed her mouth as surely as his fingers had claimed her body.

Deep inside him was a triumph he couldn't deny. Something truthful in Jim exulted.

*I'm the first. I'm the only one.*

Passion stormed him anew, and he trembled with the effort of restraint.

"What, Jim?" she whispered. "What's wrong?"

"Nothing, Sarah. Nothing at all."

When Jim thought there were no more surprises left, Sarah proved him wrong. The sweet tender woman he'd seen dancing in her garden became a fierce, fiery hoyden.

"I want everything, Jim. I want it all."

To prove her point, she moved strongly against him,

and Jim had to clench his jaw to keep from opening the floodgates and pouring out his passion.

Instead he bent down and closed his mouth over her.

Paradise came so quickly.

Sarah had never dreamed she would find it, never imagined that it would appear in the close confines of a small bed in the hold of a cabin cruiser.

She felt newborn. She was flying without wings, sailing without sails, dreaming without sleep.

Sensations bombarded her in such swift succession she could barely keep up with them. The sweet tender pleasure she'd known earlier became a wild erotic journey into unknown territory that blasted every logical thought from her mind.

She held nothing back. He carried her on a journey that spiraled toward the stars and left her shimmering there, whispering his name, begging for something she couldn't describe.

"Jim?" Her body trembled from stem to stern. She had melted all the way down; she was going to explode.

"Now, Sarah, now."

Her body needed no urging. He shot her toward the stars, and when she crash-landed, he was there to catch her. She fell straight into his arms, newborn body, enlarged heart and all.

He brushed her damp hair back from her forehead, and when he looked into her eyes, he gave her a star. That's how bright he was, how fierce, how wonderful.

"Oh, Jim…" She let her smile say what words could not.

"The rest of it is even better."

"What could be better than paradise?"

## Chapter Ten

Jim taught her to fish.

With the anchor down and the boat rocking gently on the water, he stood behind Sarah and showed her how to cast, how to play out the line, how to land the lure in exactly the right spot. She laughed and listened and learned.

"You're a natural, Sarah. Are you sure you've never done this?"

Her skin was still flushed from her intimate discoveries, her eyes still bright, her color still high.

"Never. This is my first time."

"I'm glad I'm the one to teach you," he said, and both of them knew he wasn't talking about fishing.

Jim bent down and kissed the side of her throat, and it was as thrilling as the first time he'd ever touched her. With Sarah, everything felt like the first time. He'd never fished until today. He'd never touched a woman intimately until today. Never kissed until there was Sarah.

*Never walked. Until there was Sarah.*

The memory of that day on the campus of Southside jolted Jim. He hadn't thought about it until today. He'd been too busy walking, too caught up in the sheer joy of being on his own two feet again.

But there it was. The bald truth. If it hadn't been for the threat to Sarah Sloan, Jim might never have walked.

Chills ran down his spine. *Somebody walking on your grave,* Delta always said.

Somebody or something. And the thing was Jim's conscience. Here he was—an out-of-work aviator sitting in an old boat with a fishing pole in one hand and an almost deflowered virgin in the other. The heroic image he'd held of himself while he was in her arms died a slow and painful death.

He had absolutely nothing to give her. Nothing to offer her. He was a man without a future. He didn't even have a plan.

*I'm sorry,* he'd said, and he would say it again.

She was looking at him with such shining expectation that Jim wanted to weep. More than that, he wanted her. Scoundrel that he was. He wanted to throw Sarah over his shoulder like some damned caveman and take her back into his cabin and spend the rest of the evening and the better part of the night making love to her.

It would be so easy. She wouldn't say no. Especially not after what had already happened. If looks were any indication, she would welcome him eagerly.

Desire struggled with conscience. It was a long and bitter battle, but conscience finally won.

He couldn't, and he *wouldn't* carry her back to his bed. Chivalry had taken hold of him. A little too late, regretfully, but nonetheless Jim Standing Bear wasn't about to engage this sweet trusting woman in a frivolous affair. Or any affair at all, for that matter.

Standing on tiptoe she kissed him softly on the lips.

"Thank you for being my teacher, Jim."

God, how he wanted this woman! He balled his hands into fists to keep from touching her.

"You're welcome."

Sarah gave him a strange look. He'd sounded like an uptight, self-righteous martyr. She deserved better than that.

She deserved better than him.

Cupping her face, he kissed her sun-warmed cheek.

"It was my pleasure, Sarah." He caught up their poles and handed one to her. "Now, let's fish. Otherwise we won't have any dinner."

Sarah was a good sport. She fell cheerfully into the task of pulling dinner from the sea. Later, when they cooked their catch over a fire Jim built on the beach, she maintained her good humor. She even told him stories that made him laugh.

One concerned a friend of hers from college who had gone down to La Joya to work at Sarah's school as a volunteer for the summer.

"She came without knowing a speck of the language," Sarah said. "But what she didn't know of Spanish, she made up for with her enthusiasm. One evening as we sat around a campfire roasting marshmallows, Carlos brought out his guitar and began to play."

Jim watched her face while she talked. It was expressive and lovely, a moveable feast. He wanted to kiss her moonlit cheeks and her sparkling eyes. He wanted to devour her lush lips.

Instead he took a firm grip on the spit that held their fish and an even firmer one on his emotions.

"That sounds like a great evening," he said.

"It was. And it got even better."

Sarah tilted her head slightly back when she laughed, exposing her slender throat, the throat that tasted of sunshine and roses. Jim pretended an interest in a falling star.

The whole damned sky could have fallen and he would never have noticed. That's how Sarah filled his vision. That's how she crowded out everything else in his landscape.

Sarah sucked in her breath at the sight of the blazing star, then when Jim didn't comment, she continued her story.

"As Carlos played, his audience began to clap and sing, in Spanish, of course, and I could see Janice building up to one of her wild enthusiasms. Suddenly she was up, dancing an improvised flamenco, clapping like mad and shouting, '*Grande! Grande!*'"

Jim burst out laughing, and Sarah joined him.

"You speak Spanish, I see."

"Some. Enough to get by."

"Then you know the rest of the story."

"I'd rather hear you tell it."

"Well, the entire crowd came to a standstill. 'What?' Janice asked. 'What did I say?' 'Janice,' I told her, 'you said *big.*' 'That's exactly what I meant,' she said. Janice was always one to have the last word."

"That's a great story. Tell me how you ended up in Mexico, Sarah?"

"Initially I went because of Dad. After he retired

he went to La Joya to help establish a free medical clinic. There is a crying need in that little mountain town for doctors. Teachers, too. I joined Dad one summer, fell in love with the children, and stayed.''

''You loved it, didn't you?''

''Yes. I would still be there if Dad hadn't gotten sick.''

She helped him serve the fish on picnic plates, and when their hands touched she smiled at him.

''I'm glad I didn't stay.''

''The fish is ready,'' he said.

Sarah didn't need a guidebook to tell her something was wrong. Every time she made reference to what had happened on the boat, even in the most discreet way, Jim became as inaccessible as a bank vault.

''Would you like to eat here, Sarah, or on the boat?''

''Here. Definitely.'' She bit her lower lip. ''Unless you would prefer dining onboard.''

''No, this is great.''

Jim spread the beautiful native American blanket that she loved, and then sat down as far away from her as he could get. It didn't matter that he was smiling. It didn't matter that he was pleasant. The emotional distance between them was so great he might as well have been on Mars.

The moon was putting on a spectacular display. Wouldn't it be romantic to lie on the blanket and hold each other close? Maybe she should tell Jim. Or was that too bold?

Sarah had no skills in courtship, so she did what felt natural; she reached out to take Jim's hand. He gave her hand a brief squeeze, then got up to stir the fire.

Sarah sighed. There would be no returning to paradise on the beach in the moonlight.

Not tonight. Maybe not ever.

"It's getting late," Jim said, although Sarah could tell by the position of the moon that it wasn't even close to being late.

"We should be heading back."

"Yes," she said.

What else was there to say? They loaded their picnic supplies onto the boat then rode a path of silver all the way across the bay.

Moonlight carved Jim as he stood at the wheel, and Sarah studied him until every detail was imprinted in her mind. Here was the man who had opened an entirely new world of pleasure to her. Here was the man who had chained his own desire in order to save her virtue. Here was her hero.

Sarah was falling deeply, irrevocably in love with him. And already it had the earmarks of disaster. A man like Jim Standing Bear deserved better than plain, inexperienced Sarah.

A man like Jim Standing Bear...

Sarah sighed.

"What's wrong, Sarah?"

"Nothing."

*Everything.* For surely Jim Standing Bear was going to break her heart.

At her doorway, Jim gave Sarah a chaste peck on the cheek. She was achingly beautiful with her lips softly parted and the moonlight in her hair.

So much temptation.

If he didn't get away from her quickly, he wouldn't be responsible for what might happen. He was fresh out of nobility. A quart low on restraint. Completely incapable of control.

Softly, she touched his face. "Good night, Jim."

The sweet smell of roses was on her skin, the warm blush of passion on her face. Jim needed a reprieve. He needed a cold shower. And he desperately needed a plan.

He'd promised never to hurt her. Always to be her friend.

How was he going to do that when the very sight of her made him weak with longing? How was he going to keep promises and his sanity, both?

She was smiling wistfully up at him, and he couldn't bear to leave her. Not yet.

*One more taste,* he told himself. *A kiss to remember her by.*

He cupped her face, then gently ran his fingers across her cheekbones, along the determined line of her jaw, over her lush lips. Her tongue flicked out and wet the tips of his fingers. And Jim died inside.

What would have happened if he'd made love to her, totally and completely? Would she still be looking at him with such shining expectation? Would he still be able to walk away from her with his heart intact?

His heart *was* intact. He had to keep telling himself that.

"Thank you for a beautiful day, Sarah."

"I loved every minute of it." Her blush deepened.

*Leave now. While you still can.*

Jim parted her lips with his finger, then lowered his mouth over hers. She kissed him sweetly, tenderly, deeply, but he wasn't kissing her back. He was memorizing her. Branding her.

And letting her go.

Whatever happened, he would at least have this—a goodbye he would remember the rest of his life.

## Chapter Eleven

Unable to sleep, Jim prowled his rooftop, thinking. By morning he still had no answers, only more questions. More uncertainty about his future.

The only thing he was certain about was Sarah: he had to find his way back to the beginning, back to the time when he was nothing more to Sarah Sloan than neighbor and friend.

And for that he needed the wisdom of Solomon.

In the wee hours of the morning, he sat down at his desk and wrote her a letter.

Sarah thanked her lucky stars that she didn't have to teach today. Instead she had the whole day to herself, an entire twenty-four hours to savor every last detail of her time on the boat with Jim.

In spite of the way he'd acted afterward, she still had hope. She took the cordless phone into the bathroom, in case he called while she was in the tub. She took it out to the garden in case he called while she was having breakfast. She graded her papers in the den right next to the phone.

In case he called.

Nothing was more exhausting than false hope. That's what she decided at the end of the day. She kissed her father good-night, then fell into bed like somebody dead.

When the sitter shook her awake at midnight, it took Sarah a while to become oriented.

"Your father's missing."

"What happened?"

Sarah flung back her covers and fumbled on the floor for her shoes.

"I had to go to the bathroom, and when I came back he was not in his bed. I've looked all over the house, and I can't find him."

"I think I know where he might be. Mrs. Grimes, you check the house again, just to make sure."

Sarah found him wandering around in the garden.

"Dad?"

"I can't find Ginger. She's been gone a long time. Do you know where she is?"

Guilt slashed Sarah. She'd been in her own world for two days, and to her father that was an eternity.

"It's all right. Ginger's here now."

"Listen. The orchestra's playing the rhumba." He grinned like a little kid, then swept her into the Latin rhythm.

"I've missed you, Ginger."

"I've missed you, too, Fred," she said, and she meant it.

Sometimes there was great comfort in pretending to be somebody else.

When Sarah got home on Tuesday afternoon, Savannah was in the library dancing with her father, and Delta was waiting for her with a letter from Jim and a cup of hot tea.

"I thought you might need this." She handed the tea to Sarah.

"That sounds foreboding, Delta."

"I don't know nothing about no foreboding. All I know is that man who wrote it is over yonder behind that hedge acting like a sore-tail cat."

"Is anything wrong?"

"Nothing a good dose of common sense wouldn't cure."

"Thanks for the tea, Delta. It's the perfect thing after a long day at school."

Sarah went upstairs to the privacy of her bedroom, set her tea on the bedside table, then ripped open her letter.

"Dear Sarah," she read. "As you know, Archie will be in my custody during the school hours until the end of the semester. Under the circumstances I think it best if I don't come to Southside anymore."

"No," Sarah whispered. "Please, no."

She closed her eyes, willing the last line to go away, but when she opened them it was still there. She took a bracing sip of tea that turned out not to be bracing at all.

Then she continued to read.

"Please know that I have not forgotten your boys. I will speak to Commander Sayers about sending a replacement for my Wednesday/Friday commitment. I hope I can always be here for you as your neighbor and your friend. Jim Standing Bear.''

Thunderstruck, Sarah sat on her bed staring at the letter while her tea got cold and her temper got hot. Flinging the letter aside, she marched to the kitchen to find Delta.

''I'm going out for a little while. If you need me, I'll be next door.''

''Mmm-hmm. Looks like the Bear's done met his match.''

Jim saw her coming. How could he help it? He'd been prowling his library hoping to catch a glimpse of her ever since she got home from school.

He could tell by the way she walked that Sarah Sloan was a one-man war party. Excitement grabbed him by the throat and wouldn't let go. Excitement and desire. He hung on to the former and tried to squelch the latter.

Sarah didn't come through his hedge: she stormed through. If she wanted a fight, she'd come to the right person.

Jim thanked his lucky stars that Archie had already gone home, then went downstairs to answer his doorbell. He swung open the door, and the desire gut-punched him.

*So much for control.*

''Hello, Sarah.''

''Under what circumstances?'' she asked.

Jim took that as a storm warning. When Sarah, the soul of politeness and decorum, didn't return a greeting, he'd better batten the hatches.

''I see you got my letter. Won't you come in?'' He smiled at her. In a fashion that was merely friendly, he hoped. "Or would you rather eviscerate me on my doorstep?"

"You're not going to make me laugh," she said.

Sarah followed him inside to the kitchen, which he decided was a far safer place than the den with all that comfortable furniture and all those uncomfortable memories.

"Can I get you anything?" he asked, and Sarah almost forgot herself. She almost said, *"Yes. You."*

Instead she sat down on one of his hard kitchen chairs, and crossed her legs and tugged at her skirt and tried her best to hold on to the rage that had sent her across their yards, jet-propelled.

"Yes, thank you," she said. "Tea."

"Hot or cold?"

"I like it hot."

"I do, too."

His eyes snared hers, and she fought the blush she could feel rising. Neither one of them was talking about tea. Not by a long shot.

Why couldn't she have been born the kind of girl who could have a free and easy affair that had nothing whatsoever to do with the heart? Why hadn't she been born irresistible to bears, one in particular?

Sarah squelched a sigh. She might as well be wishing for the moon.

When he turned his back to put the tea up to steep, she did her darnedest to regain a bit of her equilibrium.

"Tell me, Jim, what are the circumstances that warrant such a drastic measure?"

"I don't see substituting Chuck Sayers as a drastic measure. In fact, it will probably be a marked improvement."

"You didn't answer my question."

When he came to the table with two cups of steaming tea, he was smiling.

"You sound like a schoolmarm."

Looked like one, too. And that was the problem. That and her darned virginity. She wished she'd given in to Aubrey Clemmons when she was seventeen and full of ideals and he was eighteen and full of hormones. If she had she wouldn't be sitting in the Bear's kitchen talking about problems. She'd be in his bed. Which is exactly where she wanted to be.

In spite of the letter. In spite of his misplaced nobility. In spite of her mission.

"Drink your tea, Sarah, before it gets cold."

She wasn't the least bit interested in tea. She wanted to know why he didn't want to come to Southside and why he'd written a letter instead of coming over, and why he was sitting as far away from her as he could get.

"I think you're making a terrible mistake, Jim. You're good for the boys." She took a sip of tea. "And I think they're good for you."

She saw her error the minute the words were out of her mouth. Jim transformed from a smiling man to a grizzly.

"I don't need a rescuer, Sarah. I never did."

"I'm not trying to rescue you. I'm trying to rescue my boys."

Anger flared between them as quick and hot as their passion. The air around them sizzled. Caught in the floodlights of Jim's intense scrutiny, Sarah could do nothing but listen to her own uneven breathing and feel the runaway pounding of her heart.

"I'm offering you an alternate way of achieving your goal, Sarah. What's so bad about that?"

She couldn't bear it anymore—the raw hunger, the hopeless yearning, the aching uncertainty. Something inside her snapped.

"I'll tell you what's so bad about that, Jim Standing Bear."

She got up so fast the table rocked and her tea spilled over into the china saucer.

"You would never have written that letter if things had been different on your boat."

"Now, wait a minute, Sarah—"

"I'm not finished. Let me finish."

"By all means."

The cold courtesy of his tone was a red flag. She not only ignored it, she kicked it out of her way.

"None of this would be happening if it weren't for my unfortunate virginity."

"Your innocence is not unfortunate. It's charming and refreshing."

"If it's all that refreshing and charming, why are you running in the other direction as fast as you can?"

"I would hardly call getting a substitute for a legitimate reason running away."

Instead of placating her, his maddening calm goaded her.

"Why is it that Archie didn't become a *legitimate* reason until after I turned out to be such a disappointment?"

His face was thunderous as he came around the table. He gripped her shoulders and dragged her so close she was within inches of him. A few heartbreaking inches that might as well have been miles.

"Don't you ever think of yourself in that way again, do you hear me? Don't you ever think you have to give yourself to a man in order to be considered exciting.''

His fingers bit into her shoulders and a muscle ticked in the side of his clenched jaw.

"I know what I am, Jim. I've always known."

"I don't think you have any idea, Sarah. You're a kind, intelligent, substantive woman. A million Bethany Lawrences couldn't hold a candle to you."

Although he was heaping accolades on her and she knew she should be pleased and satisfied, she wasn't. He had left out some significant words, words like *desirable* and *passionate*. And that stung.

Sarah was tired of being the kind of woman who carried a cake next door. She wanted to be the woman who licked icing off Jim's fingers. She was tired of being the woman who was protected. She wanted to be the woman who was ravished.

And so, in spite of the way being close to Jim made her feel, in spite of the way his eyes gleamed when he looked at her, in spite of the way she longed to close the small gap between them and fall shamelessly into his arms, Sarah held on to her anger. It was her only salvation.

"If I'm so worthy why do the Bethany Lawrences get pledges of everlasting love and I get letters avowing undying friendship?" She raked her hair back from her hot face. "Don't bother to answer. I already know the answer."

"Would you be so kind as to inform me? I haven't a clue.

The Jim Standing Bear she knew would never sound so British and stuffy. She'd made him mad. *Good.* So was she.

"Because I'm not your type. I've seen pictures of

you and that…that woman. I know your type. You go
for women with cheekbones like knifeblades and two
tons of makeup.''

''And what else do I go for?''

His face thunderous, he closed in on her. Alarmed,
Sarah took a step back. She might be in retreat, but
she wasn't ready to quit the battlefield. She'd come
across the hedge spoiling for a fight, and by George
she was going to get her pound of flesh.

''Women who know how to…you know, the sophisticated kind who know all the latest *techniques*.''
His eyes gleamed with mischief and he looked as if
he would burst out laughing at any minute. Sarah got
even madder.

''See, that's just what I mean,'' she yelled. ''You
would never laugh at a woman who…who…''

Suddenly she ran out of steam. It was simply too
much effort to be mad at a man so outrageously gorgeous who looked as if he wanted to kiss her. Too
much effort and too confusing.

''You mean the brittle, shallow women who are a
dime a dozen, the women who aren't worthy to tie
your shoelaces?''

Sarah was almost in his arms, and Jim's control was
almost in shreds. He held on to the tatters with Herculean effort.

She must never know how much he wanted to kiss
her. She must never see how much he wanted to cast
nobility aside and storm up the stairs with her.

If she said one more outrageous word he was going
to kiss her. Not just kiss her, but ravish her.

His only salvation would be in retreat and capitu-
lation.

"Sending the letter was cowardly, Sarah. I should have come over."

He'd thought she would be triumphant. Instead she grew soft. The look she gave him would have melted ice caps. Jim reined in his galloping desire.

"You're no coward," she whispered, her voice and her face softened.

She moved closer, so close the full length of her body brushed against his. Her lips were only a whisper away. All he had to do was bend down and take them.

Then all would be lost. Jim had to let go. Completely. But she wasn't the one he had to prove it to. He had to prove it to himself.

"All right, Sarah. You win." He released her, then lifted his teacup. "A toast. To the woman who storms the cave of a bear in order to get what she wants."

"What did I win?" she asked.

"You won two days of my time for your boys." He smiled at her. "Again."

She was solemn when she lifted her teacup, and Jim was thrown off base.

"To victory. For my boys."

He stared at her over the rim of his cup, trying to figure her out. But she was giving away nothing. Sarah Sloan, whose emotions were always plainly written on her face, was a sphinx.

And Jim was fascinated. Silently he calculated the number of weeks till the end of the spring semester. Three weeks. And they would be the longest in his life.

If he could survive them with his honor intact, he could survive anything.

"Thanks for the tea, Jim. And thanks for agreeing to come back to Southside."

Sarah carried her cup to the sink, and Jim made a move to escort her to the door. She waved him away.

"Don't bother to see me out. I know the way."

It was best that she leave this way, Jim told himself. Best without long goodbyes. In the doorway of the kitchen, she turned back to him.

"By the way, Jim, you don't have to worry about me when you come to Southside. Once I've turned the boys over to you, I'll be busy with other things."

Sarah gave him a wistful smile and a little two-fingered wave.

"Goodbye, my friend," she said softly, and then was out the door. Out of his life.

He had won.

Wasn't that what he wanted? To be Sarah's friend and nothing more?

Jim picked up his teacup. It was empty and so was his victory.

## Chapter Twelve

Jim and Archie were slowly building a bond of trust. The silver was spread on the kitchen table, and Jim was explaining the intricacies of polish and rag.

"I'll be back from Southside in a couple of hours. If you finish the silver before then, start writing your book report."

"It's not due till next week." Archie took one look at Jim, then saluted. "Yessir, Commander." His smile showed how far he had come in a week. "You trust me with all this silver?"

"Yes."

"How do you know I won't pawn it and run off to Miami?"

"If there's anything left when Delta gets through with you, I take scalps."

When Jim left the kitchen, Archie was studiously

polishing the silver, his tongue caught between his front teeth in concentration.

Jim was headed out the door when Delta's voice stopped him in his tracks.

"You going down to that devil school of Sarah's?"

"Yes."

Delta descended on him, mop in hand. From the looks of her face, she would like to use it on his backside instead of the floor.

"I hope you're fixing to make up to Sarah for whatever you done on that boat."

Jim stiffened. Surely Sarah had not told Delta.

"You look like a long-tailed cat in a roomful of rocking chairs."

"I have to go, Delta. I don't want to be late."

"I ain't finished with you yet." Delta blocked his exit with a mop. "I don't know what happened that day, and I don't want to know. All I know is that Sarah's done got her hands full with that poor old daddy of hers trying to run away ever night of this world. When she ain't in that garden dancing with him when she ought to be sleeping, she's trying to act like she ain't been crying."

The thought of Sarah in tears broke Jim's heart. He felt like the worst kind of human being. At a time when Sarah needed him most, he was pulling away.

In protecting her by putting emotional distance between them, Jim had left her alone and vulnerable.

"I'm sorry she's having such a hard time, Delta, and I can assure you that I'll do everything in my power to help her."

"Humph. Some folks ain't got the sense of a last year's bird nest," she muttered, whacking her mop against the sides of the bucket. "Help her, my foot. If you ask me, what ought to be happening is two good people getting together 'stead of one sitting over yonder behind that fence pining and the other over here acting like God's done told him somethin' nobody else is 'posed to know.''

"'Bye, Delta. If I get any more messages, you'll be the first to know.''

"You get on out of here, Bear, before I take this mop and whop some sense into you.''

Jim got in his car, then sat there wondering what he would say when he saw Sarah Sloan. The mere sound of her name socked him like a well-placed left hook. What would it be like to see her again? To smell her sweet fragrance? To touch her?

"No.''

Jim slammed his fist into the steering wheel. The last thing in the world he intended to do was touch Sarah Sloan. Even in the name of friendship. There was only so much pain a man could bear.

Sarah looked at the clock. For the hundredth time, she guessed. Maybe more. Ten more minutes and Jim would be in her classroom.

She clenched her hands under her desk so her students wouldn't see. Thank goodness for her boys. She would have some buffer between her and Jim, however fragile.

The ticking of the clock sounded like a time bomb. Nine minutes and counting.

Oh, God, what would she say? What would she do?

Memories swamped her...the way the boat had rocked in the water, the way Jim had known exactly what she wanted, what she *needed*.

She needed Jim. She might as well have needed an ice cake from the top of Mount Everest.

Groaning, Sarah massaged her temples. On the front seat, Jared laid down his pencil.

"What's wrong, Miss Sloan?"

"Headache," she said. It was the first time she'd ever lied to her students.

*Pull yourself together*, she said. Drawing a deep breath, she took her own advice. Then, suddenly, Jim Standing Bear was at her door, and Sarah's composure went out the window.

"Good morning, Sarah."

"Hello," she said, or had she merely sighed?

Jim's eyes burned briefly through her, and when he walked into the room her students stood and applauded.

Sarah felt as if she'd personally won the Nobel peace prize. He walked to the front of the room and she could hardly see him for the mists in front of her eyes.

"What happened on this campus last week is never going to happen again." Jim made eye contact with each boy in the class before continuing. "We're going to play ball today, and we're going to play by the rules. There are only two: respect and cooperation. Stand up and repeat the rules."

One by one the boys stood.

"Louder," Jim said. "I didn't hear you." He waited for the response. "Good. You can sit down. The same rules apply to life, and starting today we're not only going to play ball by the rules, we're going to live by the rules. Stand up and tell Miss Sloan what they are."

They did as they were told, and they did it with

respect. Which was exactly what Sarah had expected. Jim Standing Bear was not a man to be taken lightly. By anybody.

She'd been right to ask his help with her boys.

Or had she?

"Now, get your things together and let's play ball," Jim said, then as the boys stored books and got out sports equipment he leaned over Sarah's desk.

She was electrified.

Did love always make a person crazy? There was that word again. The word she'd tried to stomp out, shove out, wash out, tear out of her mind.

She absolutely *refused* to love a man who didn't love her back. After all, she had her pride.

"You did a great job, Jim," she told him. "I'm glad you're back. For the boys' sake."

"If you're happy with my performance, that's good enough for me."

"I'm *very* happy with your performance," she said, and then to her mortification she blushed.

Thankfully, Jim pretended not to notice. Instead, he reached for her hand.

"Delta told me about your father, Sarah. I'm sorry."

Compassion always moved Sarah to tears. In an effort to get control of herself, she blinked back the tears and took back her hand. It didn't help one bit.

She was still a thirtysomething schoolmarm falling to pieces because the man she was falling in love with could offer her nothing but tea and sympathy. Wouldn't it be lovely if he also offered a big strong shoulder to cry on? A beautifully sculpted chest to lean on? A wonderful pair of arms to hide in?

Even for a little while. Sarah wasn't the kind of woman to hide from a problem forever.

"If there is any way I can help you with your father, please let me know. I mean that sincerely, Sarah."

"Thank you, Jim. I appreciate that."

The sounds of tennis shoes slapping wooden floors and boys' chatter filled the room. Then one by one her students filed out, and Sarah was left alone with Jim still leaning over the edge of her desk, his face fierce, his eyes burning like twin coals.

She drew a ragged breath. She was not herself. All this tension combined with her sleepless nights was wearing her down. She felt as if somebody else had taken over her skin, somebody who was going to cry at any minute.

She was absolutely, positively not going to cry in front of Jim. Tears would only prove to him that she was somebody who needed protecting.

Why didn't he just go away? Why hadn't she left the classroom the minute he came in?

"The boys are probably waiting for you, Jim."

"Probably."

Why did he still linger? And why did she want him to?

"I suppose I should go."

"Yes."

"You aren't coming?"

"No. I have papers to grade."

"Why don't you spend this free time in the teacher's lounge, Sarah? You look as if you could use some rest."

"I don't need a keeper, Jim."

She jerked open her drawer and slapped her files on the desk. For a moment Jim looked as if he were going to argue with her. Instead he left the room. *Stalked out* would be a better terminology.

Sparks flew every time the two of them were in the same room. Unfortunately, they were sparks of anger.

Barricaded behind brick walls, Sarah spent the next fifteen minutes blindly shuffling papers. Finally, she couldn't stand it any longer. She had to see Jim or die.

She went to the bookcase where she could appear to be browsing while she was gazing at the view through the window.

"Like a spy," she said, disgusted at her own foolishness.

That was another thing. Being around Jim Standing Bear made her giddy. Even Julie had noticed—though, thank goodness, she hadn't noticed anything else.

On the ball court, Jim was going one-on-one with Jared, running, dribbling, pivoting, shooting. Sarah watched, fascinated. She'd read every word she could find about Jim. Because he was a Blue Angel, the news media had printed every detail they could find about his accident.

Sarah knew the kind of car he'd been driving. She knew where he'd been going. She knew the number and type of surgeries he'd had.

Here was a man with pins in his knees, a man who'd had his right shoulder broken, his spleen removed, his upper arm crushed and both wrists fractured.

He had a superb body. The body of an athlete…and a top-notch aviator. In spite of the slowed reflexes, the occasional halt in his step, there was beauty and grace in the way he moved.

There was something else, too, a pain he tried to hide behind a carefully set expression. Every play he made came at great cost to Jim.

Riveted, Sarah watched. She knew the sacrifice he'd made in coming here when he didn't really want to be around her. Changing his mind after he'd written the letter had probably cost him a bit of pride.

What she hadn't realized was the physical cost.

She couldn't hide while the man she loved suffered. She had to do something, even if it was nothing more than simply being there. Sarah dashed to her desk, grabbed a sheaf of papers, then raced outside to the ball court.

Jim came over to the sidelines.

There was a fine sheen of sweat on his face, and his damp T-shirt stuck to his body in ways so enticing Sarah had to swallow a lump in her throat.

"I changed my mind," she said.

"Great."

His smile dazzled her. For a moment the air between them shimmered with magic, then Jim broke contact.

"Good," he amended. "I'm glad to have a friend in my cheering section."

Sarah kept her smile in place until he was back on the court playing ball.

She figured that if she'd set out to be an actress instead of a dancer, she'd be famous by now.

It was the last day of school and Jim figured he deserved a medal. For three weeks he'd come to Southside and coached Sarah's boys without once giving in to his urge to touch her.

Day after day Sarah looked more exhausted, more stressed. Her dad was getting increasingly worse.

Delta had told him. Not Sarah. Around Jim she kept up a cheerful facade. She was shutting him out.

What had he expected? Wasn't that what he'd wanted?

He knew she had to get up night after night to find her father in the garden. Delta had told him.

Jim didn't go to his rooftop anymore. He had forfeited the right to watch Sarah dancing in the moonlight.

"Jim?"

Sarah touched him lightly on the arm. They were standing in the hallway waiting for her boys to line up for graduation from Southside.

"Thank you for coming today. You didn't have to, you know."

"I wanted to be here, Sarah. For Archie, for the other boys."

*For you,* he thought, but he didn't dare say it aloud. His feelings were too raw. Hers, too fragile.

"Archie wouldn't be here if it weren't for you."

"I did what I could. I hope it was enough."

"I worry about that, Jim. Not only for Archie, but for the rest of my boys, too. What will happen to them this summer? What will happen to them when they enter high school next year? Have we done enough?"

"You certainly have, Sarah. I've watched you pour your heart and soul into these boys. My contribution has been small."

"The boys have been honored by your presence, Jim. And so have I."

In the distance they could hear Betty Jane Crocker strike the first chord of "Pomp and Circumstance." Sarah's boys stood all in a row, their faces shining from the unaccustomed scrubbing and from pride.

"Better hurry, Miss Sloan," Jared said. "You gonna miss the graduation."

"I wouldn't miss the graduation for anything in the world."

Sarah smiled at her boys, then held out her hand to Jim.

"Thank you again, Jim. For everything."

He watched her walk away, watched her weave her way through the crowd, proud and tall, her head high, her back straight.

He would have still been watching if Archie hadn't caught his attention.

"Coach? I want to thank you for all you done...*did* for me."

Jim clapped the boy on the shoulder. "I'm going to miss you, Archie," he said, meaning it. "You take care of yourself this summer, and stay out of trouble. I want to see you in regular high school next year, and I want you to stay there."

The boy blinked back tears. "Ain't nobody...*hadn't* nobody ever cared what I done before you and Miss Sloan."

"She's a great lady."

"Yeah, Coach, she is."

Betty Jane Crocker gave the musical cue, and the boys began the processional. Archie saluted as he passed by Jim, and one by one the boys followed suit.

When the last boy had saluted and the last strains of the march died away, Jim slipped into the back of the auditorium for the ceremonies. He could see the back of Sarah's head, but she never turned around, never looked his way.

And when the ceremonies were over, Jim hurried from the building, got into his car and drove away. Sarah Sloan and her wounded boys were out of his life forever.

Jim couldn't bear to go home in case he accidentally caught a glimpse of Sarah next door.

In case his heart accidentally broke.

Instead he drove to the beach and thought about a future without Sarah Sloan.

"What are you going to do now that school's out?" Julie asked her.

"Sleep," Sarah said.

They were in the garden having green lemon tea and raspberry tarts Julie had picked up at the bakery on the way to Sarah's house.

"You should go somewhere. I'll come over and make sure everything is okay with Dad and the sitters."

"Where would I go?"

"Anywhere. London. Paris. New York, for goodness sakes."

The thought of being alone in those cities, or any city for that matter, filled Sarah with sadness. If she was going to be by herself, she'd rather do it right at home.

"I have an idea. Why don't I go with you? George can check on Dad."

"Oh, I don't know." She glanced toward Jim's house, but there was no sign of the Bear.

"Forget about him." Julie had always been able to read Sarah like a book. "So, he planted a few flowers in your garden. Big deal."

"You forgot about Southside. You should have seen him with the boys, Julie. He's a natural."

"Now you listen to me, Sarah." Julie took both Sarah's hands. "You've got to start thinking about

yourself once in a while. You can't spend the rest of
your life being caretaker to the world.''

"It's my work, Julie.''

"All right. But don't make it your life.'' Julie
nabbed two raspberry tarts and handed one to her sister. "I'm packing the kids off to camp next week, and
I'll be free as a breeze. It would be fun to shop at
Bloomingdale's with my sister.''

Julie reconsidered a moment, then added, ''Or if it
would make you feel better, I'll personally handle
things here while you take a break. Promise me you'll
at least think about it, Sarah.''

"All right. I promise.''

The beach was a great place to run with the sand
dragging and pulling so that every step Jim took was
the equivalent of four, he figured. Besides, the beach
was a great thinking place. There was nothing to in-
terfere with the process. All that water and fresh air.
No noise except the occasional cry of seagulls and the
soft swooshing of the surf breaking against the shore.

What he thought about most was Sarah, about how
much he missed her. With a start he realized he was
addicted to her. The two days a week at Southside had
not been a mere act of compassion for her boys; they
had been Jim's fix.

Now all he had to keep him going was an occasional
glimpse of Sarah out the window. It wasn't enough.
Not by a long shot.

He had to see her in person. He had to be close
enough to see the way her eyes turned the deep green
of summer pastures when she was happy. He had to
be close enough to inhale the heady scent that was all
her own.

He raced back to his car with that damnable hitch in his gait that no amount of running would cure, then hurried home to shower, breaking a speed limit here and there.

Something he'd never done when he was flying his Hornet. God, how he missed speed. How he missed that heart-in-throat moment of takeoff when the G forces plastered him to the seat and felt as if they would never let go.

*Don't think about it. Think about Sarah.*

In many ways, being with her was the same as take-off. There were times when she immobilized him with forces beyond his control.

Back home he showered and dressed and was ringing her doorbell in the time it normally would have taken him to shave. The door was already opening when he realized he didn't know what he was going to say, what excuse he would give for coming.

Then Sarah smiled at him, and it no longer mattered.

''Jim, how nice to see you. Won't you come in?''

It was that easy. He was in her house, breathing in her fragrance and basking in the warm glow of her smile.

She led him into the library where French doors overlooked her garden, and a copy of *Everyday Zen* lay open on a table beside a comfortable-looking chair. For some reason the cozy scene made him sad. He thought of his own den with its masculine furniture and stone fireplace and ceiling-to-floor bookshelves filled with his favorite books.

It should have been cozy, but it wasn't. Sometimes late at night he'd be reading, then suddenly look up as if expecting to see someone sitting across the room, somebody with soft skin and a soft smile, somebody with firelight shining in her dark hair. But the chair would be empty.

*You're going soft,* he'd tell himself, or worse, *getting old.*

Now he realized that wasn't true. He was lonely.

Somewhat shaken by the knowledge, he took the chair Sarah offered, then sat pondering his life while she hurried to the kitchen to get him a cup of tea.

Tea was the last thing he wanted. He wanted Sarah. It was that simple. In spite of all his noble resolutions and high-flying honor, he'd overlooked the basic truth: he was irrevocably attracted to Sarah Sloan and he could never be merely her friend.

"I know you like it hot." She gave him the teacup, then blushed as their hands touched.

Damn the tea. Jim wanted to pull her onto his lap and kiss her until the blush colored her whole face. Her whole body. He wanted to kiss her until she was rosy all over.

Instead he took his tea and she took her seat beside the window. The sun streaming through made her look like a Madonna. Jim silently cursed the sun. He didn't want to think of Sarah as virginal and untouchable.

"What have you been doing since school is out?" she asked.

"Reading, running, trying to get myself back into shape. I got fat and lazy in the wheelchair."

"Not that I noticed," she said, then blushed furiously and tried to cover with chatter. "I've been reading like crazy, too. Novels, mostly, but sometimes something like this." She held up her book on Zen. "Every year after school is out I rediscover reading for pleasure."

"What else do you do for pleasure, Sarah?"

He hadn't meant to say that, but now it was too late. The question with all its intimate overtones hovered between them like the proverbial elephant in the living room.

"I used to love to travel. Julie wants the two of us to go to New York, but I don't want to get that far away from Dad and besides, I can't seem to work up the enthusiasm she has for shopping."

Her hand flew to her mouth as if she could take back the words. It was a gesture Jim knew well, and one that always made him feel warm inside.

"I didn't mean that the way it sounded. Julie is a wonderful person, and far, far too intelligent and substantive to be mistaken for a shopaholic."

"I would never make that mistake. She's a lovely woman in every way."

"Oh, that's right. You know her. She was here when you planted the flowers." Her smile lit her whole face. "I love them. Every time I go into the garden, I think of you."

Jim basked in her praise. He couldn't help himself. Especially when her eyes turned that wonderful deep shade of emerald he loved so well.

"And Archie, too, of course."

Nothing she said could take away the warm glow that lit his whole insides, and he supposed that was why he found himself on the verge of making such a rash offer.

Alarm bells went off all over his head, but he ignored them.

"If you still have a mind to travel, you can go to New Orleans with me."

What the heck? It was a perfectly legitimate travel offer, wasn't it? Two people motoring down to New

Orleans, one for business, the other for pleasure. Sight-seeing pleasure, that is. And it was only a few hours away.

Sarah had the deliciously heated look of a woman who had just risen from a long bath. Or from a long hot afternoon in bed with her lover.

Jim's thoughts were getting more dangerous by the minute. But it was too late now.

He was in her house and the offer was on that table. If he reneged he would lose her completely.

"My brother's graduating from medical school. I'll get us a couple of rooms and you can take in the sights while I dispense brotherly advice."

His belated explanation did nothing to dim Sarah's glow.

"Why…" His blood pressure shot up ten degrees when her pink tongue flicked out and wet her lips. "I think that would be…" She did the tongue thing again, and Jim had to ram his fists into his pockets to keep from reaching for her. "…perfectly lovely."

Flying without a plane was a new experience to Jim. That's how he got home. He didn't come down until the middle of the night. And then it was a crash landing.

"How am I going to keep my hands off her for five days?"

Sarah couldn't sleep for thinking about what she'd done. She could still change her mind, she told herself. Going to New Orleans with Jim Standing Bear was not only foolish and frivolous, it was downright dangerous.

*Separate rooms,* he'd said, and that all sounded well and good till Sarah thought about the connecting door.

Then she got so deliciously hot she had to throw the covers back and march downstairs into the kitchen to make herself a big glass of lemonade. Freshly squeezed.

Mauling the lemons helped some. But not much.

She went into the library to read, but she didn't have Zen on her mind—all that stillness and contemplation. What she had on her mind wouldn't do to tell.

Especially not Julie.

Lord, what was she going to tell Julie?

"I'll think about it tomorrow," she said, then giggled at her untypical Scarlett-like response to a problem that was growing by leaps and bounds.

In the morning it would be so big Sarah would have to move out of the house to escape it. Or leave the house. As in a trip to New Orleans.

Sarah looked at the clock so she could mark the moment. At precisely 3:35 a.m. she knew that she was going to New Orleans with Jim Standing Bear.

Smiling, she sank into a blissful sleep that lasted until Delta's vacuuming woke her up. Sarah reached for the phone.

"Julie, I've decided to take that trip."

"Great. Let's stay at the Algonquin. Or would you prefer something overlooking Central Park?"

"I'm not going to New York, Julie. I'm going to New Orleans."

"Well, I've always liked that city. We'll drink lots of hurricanes and hear lots of good jazz."

*Oh, help. Now what?* She didn't want to hurt her sister's feelings, and the Bear had said he'd get *two* rooms.

Still...

Sarah's heart fell. She could hear it hit the floor and shatter like glass.

"Julie? Would you mind terribly staying here?"

That sounded awful. Julie didn't say anything, and now Sarah knew what *pregnant* silence meant.

"To see about Dad," she added, much, much too late, she feared. Sarah twisted the telephone cord until her fingers were so tangled she might never get them out. "I mean, you *did* offer, Julie. That's what you said you would do."

"Sarah, don't get yourself in a wad. Of course, I'll watch after Dad. Besides, I've been neglecting George lately. With the kiddies out of town this will give me a chance to make it up to him. Excite him a little."

Julie laughed, adding, "I think I'll go to town and buy that fabulous black lace nightie I've been drooling over. Want to come?"

"No, thanks. I have a million things to do. Bye, Julie. And thanks."

Sarah untangled herself from the telephone cord, then raced to her closet and inspected her nightwear. An assortment of old T-shirts from places like Myrtle Beach and Yellowstone National Park. She couldn't even call it lingerie. With the exception of a white gown that covered everything she had twice over, she didn't have a thing in her closet that would even classify as a gown, much less an instrument of excitement.

Especially to somebody like the Bear.

"Good grief."

What was she thinking? Certainly not of separate rooms.

## *Chapter Thirteen*

Sarah had to keep pinching herself. Here she was riding down the highway with Jim Standing Bear, talking about everything under the sun except flying.

"Are you ready?" he asked when he picked her up at her house, and she'd said, "Yes." That's how simple it had been. And how lovely. How wonderfully, unbelievably lovely.

"I feel like a bird," she said suddenly, then laughed at her own foolishness.

Jim cast a sideways glance at her and smiled.

"What kind of bird, Sarah?"

His question validated her, and she changed from feeling silly to feeling like a woman reborn, a woman with New Orleans on her horizon and a new pink silk gown in her bag—just in case.

"A crane, maybe, or a great blue heron. One of

those big birds with a wingspan about ten feet wide. Big enough to fly where they want to go.''

The water birds she'd mentioned were all along the side of the road, perching in skeletal trees hung with Spanish moss and wading in the swamp, their long legs keeping them well above the waterline.

''You've just described freedom.''

He spoke with the nostalgia of a pilot whose wings had been clipped, and he sounded so wistful, Sarah was moved to tears. She turned her face toward the car window and blinked rapidly. *Stay away from the subject of flying,* she told herself.

''I'm glad I decided to come. Thank you for inviting me, Jim. I promise not to be in your way.''

''Nonsense. The graduation ceremonies will take up a couple of hours. Ben has friends here and his own agenda. I'll be lucky to spend one evening with him.''

He swung toward her again. ''He's a great kid. I think you're going to like him.''

Sarah's heart did the fandango. Jim was including her in his plans. He was taking her to meet his brother. Sort of. What was the meaning of it all?

''If he's anything like his brother, I'm sure I will.''

That took his attention off the road again. He studied her so long the car seemed to be driving itself. She felt a telltale flush creeping into her face again. A dead giveaway of her turmoil.

There was bound to be a self-help book somewhere that would tell her how to stop blushing in ten easy steps. Or maybe somebody gave seminars on the subject—seven days to sophistication.

''Your skin is beautiful when you blush, Sarah,'' Jim said, and suddenly she wouldn't trade her flushed face for all the sophistication in the world.

She murmured a thank-you, then they both pretended to watch the scenery. The swamps gave way to service stations and fast-food restaurants and car dealerships.

"We'll soon be there," Jim said. "I found us a great place to stay in the French Quarter. On Bourbon Street."

*Separate rooms.* The thought was icy water dumped on her fire. Icy water she desperately needed. The longer she was in the car with Jim Standing Bear, the bigger her fire got.

"That's nice," she said.

"Have you ever been there, Sarah?"

"Not since I was a kid. Julie and I came down with Dad to a medical conference. We called our sitter Godzilla. She wouldn't let us do anything we wanted to, which was probably a darned good thing since Julie wanted us to go into the strip joints and I wanted to dance on a riverboat all by myself."

Her dreams spilled out like bright crystals from an overturned jar. How easy it was with Jim.

"She sounds like our house mother at the orphanage. Every time I managed to steal a cigarette when the janitor wasn't looking, she confiscated it."

Sarah laughed. "Oh, she sounds *really* mean."

Jim's stories of his childhood filled Sarah with such longing she could barely contain her sighs. She'd always wanted children of her own. She guessed that was one reason she was always so enamored of other people's kids.

"She took my slingshot, too. Of course that was after she caught me on the rooftop trying to take down the man in the moon."

"You were a handful."

He shot her another of those oblique glances. "I still am," he said, and for a shimmering moment, neither of them could look away.

Then suddenly, there was New Orleans, a city where great jazz poured from every open doorway and wonderful possibilities lurked on every corner. Sarah embraced the city with a smile.

Her smile dazzled Jim. As if riding in the car with her weren't enough. She was a good traveling companion, easy to talk to, easy to laugh with.

But that smile… He couldn't seem to look away.

It involved her whole face, not just her lips, which were delicious enough on their own. He'd spent the better part of a hundred miles wanting to kiss them.

Which was probably where that remark about being a handful came from. Way out of left field. Unexpected by both of them.

He'd better start trying to remember the purpose of this trip. Dual purposes, actually. To see Ben graduate and to give Sarah an opportunity to get away from the burdens of caretaking.

Thankfully the traffic demanded his attention, and he had no more time to consider her lush mouth nor the heady fragrance she was wearing. What was it? Something new, he thought. Not her usual light floral scent but something far more exotic, far more enticing. It was a fragrance that put him in mind of being on a beach with a full moon shining on the sand and a woman at his side.

*Sarah* at his side. Always Sarah.

It turned out that the rooms he'd booked had a connecting door. That was the first thing he'd noticed. The second was the shared balcony. Both rooms had

French doors that led to a small balcony overlooking a secluded garden, lush and still dripping from the quick rainshower that had washed the city clean just as they'd entered the French Quarter.

"Well, what do you think?" he asked Sarah.

"I think it's absolutely wonderful."

She was gazing deeply into his eyes, and he was certain that she wasn't talking about the rooms.

They had shrimp po'boys for dinner, the best she'd ever eaten, Sarah declared, then they wandered down the street to Preservation Hall where they sat cross-legged on the floor and heard jazz played the way it was meant to be, the wailing sax, the mournful trombone and the trumpet so heavenly Sarah swore to Jim that the man playing it had to be the angel Gabriel, himself.

Jim loved Cajun food, he loved jazz, he loved the French Quarter with its darkly romantic history, but most of all he loved watching Sarah Sloan enjoy the city.

*I gave her this,* he thought. *I gave her this happiness.*

And for him, it was enough. It was enough until they said good-night in the hallway with a tender clasping of hands and a brief press of their cheeks. Then he was in bed alone and nothing in the world could make him forget that Sarah was on the other side of the wall, sweeter smelling than the jasmine abloom in New Orleans's courtyards and twice as enticing.

Desire slammed him hard, and he groaned. Was that a sound he heard through the wall? Was she restless, too? Was she tangled in her sheets while she wanted to be tangled in his arms?

"Arrogant bastard," he growled. Then feeling like the bear he was, he flung back the covers and stalked toward the French doors. He had to have air. He had to have relief. Now he knew why men smoked.

Even if standing on the balcony looking at the stars didn't give him relief, at least it would give him some fresh air.

He pulled open the doors, and that's when he knew there would be no relief for him tonight, for there was Sarah, wearing a diaphanous gown the color of sunrises and a body that drove him mad.

"Oh." Her hand flew to her throat, and her exclamation came out as a long sigh.

"I didn't mean to startle you."

"I came out for some air."

"Me, too." His hand was still on the door handle. "I'll just step back inside and give you some privacy."

He meant what he said, but then his eyes got tangled up with hers and he couldn't move. He couldn't speak. He could barely breathe.

Apparently she was having the same trouble. She drew a deep shuddering breath that shifted the soft fabric over her breasts. Desire became a sledgehammer.

The only relief Jim had from passion's powerful blows was to drink her in. His gaze roamed from the lush breasts barely contained to the slender waist to the long legs clearly defined. Her entire body beckoned him through its silken covering.

Her tongue flicked out in a provocative gesture that was almost his undoing.

*Leave,* he told himself. *Leave before you do something you'll both regret.*

"Don't go," she whispered. "Oh, Jim, please don't go."

Jim swept her into his arms and honor vaporized in the sultry night, leaving behind a man and a woman—and a need so great it could not be denied.

Paradise came so quickly. Sensations bombarded Sarah—the feel of Jim's lips on hers, the smell of jasmine wafting from the garden, the brightness of a moon made especially for lovers.

*Lovers.* As the word whispered through her mind, everything that was ordinary in Sarah's life vanished, and she became a new woman. A woman made to wear silk. A woman created for heady kisses in the moonlight. A woman reborn.

She was in Jim's arms her body pressed intimately against his, and there was not a virginal thought in her head. Every part of her bloomed. He deepened the kiss, and Sarah's mouth flowered open for his questing tongue.

Delicious hot-sweet tastes. Rough silk texture. Desire so raw it stripped her of everything, even the will to breathe.

The earth rolled on without her, and she was left standing on a secluded balcony unaware of anything except the man who held her in his arms. Jim Standing Bear. Her hero. Her love.

When he came up for air, he looked deep into her eyes, searching for answers.

"Yes," she whispered. "Yes."

And he picked her up and carried her into his room, straight to his bed where the sheet lay tangled and the pillows were wadded, mute evidence of his inner turmoil.

Something in Sarah exulted. The confident woman he lay down beside was not the scared woman he'd carried below deck on his boat. She stretched, langorous and sensual as a jungle cat while Jim stripped off his white T-shirt and the navy-blue pajama bottoms that made him look the ruler of a small kingdom in a country with a name nobody could pronounce.

The moon painted him a shimmering copper, and he was so wonderfully made, so completely gorgeous she wondered how this moment had ever come to pass. Then he lay down once more and began to caress her and murmur sweet endearments in a voice so tender it broke her heart, and Sarah no longer wondered. She felt beautiful. In Jim's arms she *was* beautiful.

"Make love to me, Jim," she whispered.

Lifted on one elbow, he studied her face. "Sarah? You're sure?"

"Yes." She wove her fingers in his hair and pulled him down to her. "Don't talk," she whispered. "Just love me. Love me completely."

His mouth was magic, his hands tender as he rediscovered every inch of her body. They had left the door open and from somewhere in the distance a silver horn moaned the blues.

But there were no blues in their shared bedroom that night. Only the sweet aching music of their bodies, straining toward one another.

Sarah was a piano and Jim, the virtuoso. She thrilled and hummed and vibrated to his touch, and when touch was no longer enough, when passion crashed through them insistent as cymbals, Jim rose above her, godlike, and took the thing she most wanted to give.

"Sarah?" He lifted his head and planted tender kisses all over her face. "Are you all right?"

She held him tightly to her, deep inside her body and her heart.

"Yes," she whispered. "Oh, yes." Then she smiled. "I thought I'd found paradise on your boat. I was only on the outskirts."

His smile was a thing of glory, and what followed even more glorious. It was an unforgettable symphony, a love song that would play in her heart until the day she died.

Jim woke with a start. The French door still stood wide open. It was not quite daylight. A hushed gray mist hung over the garden, and through it he could see the silhouettes of moss-draped trees.

Sarah lay curled against him, flushed and warm, one hand resting on his chest and her leg flung carelessly across his hips. A faint smile curved her lips as she slept.

*What have I done?*

A pile of pink silk on the floor and the stain on the sheet gave mute evidence. Jim felt like a thief. He'd stolen a treasure he had no right to take.

Nothing had changed in his life. Nothing except an awesome night that was seared into his brain. For a few hours the rest of the world had vanished, and he'd been heroic and invincible.

Soon the sun would shed its rays on his selfish deed and Sarah would wake up with the light gone from her eyes. Then what?

Jim wanted desperately to pace, but he didn't want to wake Sarah. Trying not to disturb her, he lay back against the sheets stiff and unyielding as a board, staring at the ceiling.

What was he going to do when she woke up?

His mind was a squirrel cage, but none of the thoughts running around seemed to be a logical solution.

Sarah stirred. First she stretched in a leisurely fashion. Then her hand started a slow, sensuous journey down his body, and suddenly desire was a thoroughbred champing at the bit, stamping to get out of the gate.

Jim bit back a groan. Or maybe he didn't. Sarah lifted herself on one elbow and smiled down at him.

"What we did was wonderful, Jim. Do you think we could do it again?"

Pure joy flooded him and when he reached for her, he looked directly into her eyes. The light was still there. Brighter than ever.

And Jim became a hero all over again.

It was almost noon before they got out of bed.

"I feel absolutely decadent," Sarah said, laughing. "And totally wonderful."

Jim felt as if medals had been pinned on his chest. "I'm going to call Ben and tell him we'll be a little late for lunch."

"I'll hurry."

"No need. Take your time. And Sarah..." She was standing in the doorway, her body flushed as pink as the gown that dangled from her hand. "You might as well leave the connecting door open."

"I'm so glad you said that."

When Sarah disappeared into her room, Jim caught

sight of himself in the mirror. The grin on his face looked permanent.

Sarah worried privately all the way to the restaurant about meeting Jim's brother. What if he didn't like her? What if she didn't know what to say to him? What if he found her boring, or worse yet, completely wrong for his brother?

She told none of this to Jim. For one thing, her worries were the concerns of a woman in love. And Jim hadn't said the first thing about love. Meeting the family of the man you loved was quite different from meeting the family of a good friend.

Sarah slid a glance at Jim. Only four more days and they would be back in Pensacola living in separate houses, sleeping in separate beds.

Or would they? Last night had been a miracle. What if another one occurred? What if he fell in love with her? Was there a way to make that happen?

She glanced at the St. Louis Cathedral as they passed by. While she was here she might just duck inside and light a candle to love. It couldn't hurt, could it?

"There he is," Jim said, and before Sarah had time to act like a scared rabbit, Ben Standing Bear was striding her way, smiling through the introductions, then hugging Sarah as if he'd known her all his life.

And that's how she felt about him. Sometimes it happened that way with people. An instant rapport developed so that the time spent together simply flew by.

Ben was a great raconteur. He had her laughing so hard tears rolled down her face.

"Dad would love that story. He used to tell similar ones about his days in medical school."

"Your father is a hero of mine. The medical profession has lost a great mind." Ben covered Sarah's hand with his. So like his brother, she thought. "I'm sorry, Sarah. For both your sakes."

"Thank you, Ben. You're very kind." She smiled at both of them, lingering when her eyes met Jim's. "And very much like your brother."

"Another hero of mine." Ben clapped his brother on the shoulder.

"And of mine," Sarah said softly.

Jim felt the glow all the way to his bones. Did it show? Did his brother notice?

He wasn't long in finding out. As soon as Sarah excused herself, Ben sat back in his chair and laughed.

"She's a terrific woman. Outclasses Bethany Lawrence by a country mile. Congratulations, big brother."

"For what?"

"You've picked a winner this time."

"Look, Ben, it's not what you think. We're neighbors and good friends and..."

"And?"

"The rest is none of your business."

"Yes, it is. If she's going to be my sister-in-law, I have a perfect right to pry."

"You're way off base, Ben. I told you we're just very good friends."

"All I can say is it's a damned good thing you're so handsome because I certainly got all the brains in the family."

After lunch the three of them went to the zoo, and just as they parted company it began to rain.

"I'll get a cab," Jim said.

"I love this." Sarah lifted her face and raindrops caught in her eyelashes. "Can we walk awhile in the rain, Jim?"

"For you, anything."

That's what he had wanted to do anyway. Leaning down he kissed the raindrops off her face, and then because she was so close and so appealing, he took possession of her rain-slicked lips.

He'd meant it to be a brief kiss, but it turned into a passionate embrace that lasted until they were both soaked. They clung to each other, then joined hands and walked down St. Charles Avenue laughing.

"Oh, look, Jim. There's a streetcar. Can we ride?"

"It must be the one called desire."

She gazed at him, radiant and flushed, and he kissed her again before swinging her aboard the car. The only other passenger was an old man holding a small dog that matched his long red beard.

Jim and Sarah sat in the back of the car holding hands. He wondered how life could possibly get better. Laughing up at him, she licked a drop of rain off her lips, and he leaned over to whisper, "I know a wonderful way to spend the rest of a rainy afternoon."

"Oh," she said, with a sigh.

His heart swelled three times its size, and by the time they got back to their hotel, he was wondering how he'd ever managed to get through the last few hours without making love to her.

He'd wanted her in the restaurant, watching her eat shrimp scampi. He'd wanted her in the zoo watching her delight over the baby giraffe. He'd wanted her in the rain, waiting for the streetcar. Wanted her desperately.

He started kissing her when they were barely inside the room. She leaned against the wall, breathless and glowing.

"I can't wait another minute, Sarah."

"Please don't wait, Jim."

So polite. Such a lady.

And such a delicious hoyden.

He peeled away the bit of hampering lace, then lifted her off her feet. She wrapped her legs around him and he slid home.

Much later he held her still braced against the wall, and leaned his damp forehead against hers.

"You drive me wild, Sarah."

"I've never driven a man wild."

"I'm glad."

He carried her into the bathroom where he tenderly stripped away the rest of her clothes, then his own.

"Are you ready for your bath, m'lady?"

"Only if the tub will hold two."

"It'll be a tight squeeze."

"Good."

"Minx."

They waited until the tub was brimming with hot water, then Sarah added bubble bath. Jim climbed in behind her and after much to-do they arranged their long legs so that she was mostly in the tub and only part of him draped over the edges.

Jim bathed Sarah with tender care, then he shampooed her hair.

"I've never been so pampered in my life." She swiveled around and kissed him softly on the lips. "You are the most wonderful man in the world."

Too full to reply, he dried her with a fluffy towel,

then wrapped her in the white terry-cloth robe provided by the hotel and carried her to bed.

"Rest now," he said.

And she curled against him, fragrant and sweet. Within minutes he could hear the even tone of her breathing. He pressed a tender kiss on her forehead, filled with wonder that holding a sleeping woman should feel so right.

## Chapter Fourteen

She and Jim were having breakfast at Brennan's, and if a dining experience could be called erotic, this was it. Food so rich that one bite was enough to satisfy a full-blown case of hunger and two bites seemed excessive. Not a single artificial ingredient on the menu. Real butter, thick cream, orange juice freshly squeezed then laced with enough alcohol to put a buzz in Sarah's head.

She was beginning to feel very selfish and more than a little scared. For three days she'd lived in a fantasy world. Jim pampered her, treated her to meals at the finest restaurants, accompanied her on every sightseeing trip her heart desired. But best of all, he acted as if his appetite for loving was as insatiable as her own.

She felt like a bride. Almost, she could believe she was on her honeymoon.

What was going to happen when they left New Orleans? How was she going to handle reality?

"Jim, I need to talk to you."

A look of alarm flitted across his face. "What's wrong?"

She quickly covered his hands with hers. "Nothing. Absolutely nothing."

She smiled at him, loving the way he smiled back, loving the way his dark eyes glowed when he looked at her.

"Everything is wonderful, perfect," she said.

So perfect she was afraid of waking up in her own bed and being told she'd been in a coma and everything she'd thought to be true was merely a dream.

"I'm glad, Sarah. I wanted everything to be good for you."

"It is, Jim. You've made it that way."

He kissed her fingertips, one by one, and a familiar flame leaped into his eyes. Sarah's heart melted, and she had to bite her tongue to keep from telling him she loved him.

"What do you want to do today, Sarah?" His smile became mischievous. "In addition to the obvious."

Flushed by love and uncertainty, Sarah pushed her hair back from her hot face. The hair Jim so lovingly shampooed every day.

She wanted to grab his hand and race back to their room and lock the door against the world for the rest of the day. The rest of the year. The rest of her life.

"I've been very selfish," she said. "You haven't spent a minute alone with your brother."

"He's not feeling deprived, and neither am I. He likes you and enjoys your company."

"I'm glad. I feel the same about him. Still, I want to give the two of you some time alone."

"What will you do, Sarah?"

*Be lost without you.*

"Stroll the Quarter, plunder the antique shops, things like that. Don't worry about me, Jim. I'll be fine without you."

He looked puzzled and even a little hurt, she thought. Sarah took his hand and planted a tender kiss in his palm.

"But not as fine as I am with you, Jim. I want you to know that."


"She's the sweetest woman I've ever known," Jim said after he'd recounted Sarah's conversation to his brother, leaving out the intimate parts.

They were sitting in the Café du Monde having beignets and café au lait and enjoying the breeze that had sprung up over the river.

"That's why I want to do something special for her," he added.

"How special? Give her a ring, maybe?"

Jim gave Ben a dark look meant to quell, but his brother only laughed.

"It's about damned time you settled down, big brother. I'm wanting some family."

"What do you think I am, a turnip?"

"A stubborn, clueless man. I just hope you don't wait too long."

"Too long for what?"

"Somebody else is liable to grab her, you know."

"I don't know why I ever tell you anything." Jim felt grouchy and he didn't even know why. "Are you going to help me with Sarah's surprise, or not?"

"What kind of surprise?" Ben asked, and Jim told him.

If Sarah had looked across Jackson Square she might have seen Ben and Jim, but she was intent on her mission. Standing outside the St. Louis Cathedral she felt both awed and humbled. If God couldn't hear her petitions in this establishment, then there was just no sense praying, she decided.

Taking a lace-edged handkerchief from her purse, she covered her head, then went inside. Coolness and a great echoing silence enveloped her. The church smelled of the musty relics of long-dead saints, incense and sincerity.

Not being Catholic, Sarah passed the holy water by and went directly to the altar. The wonderful thing about these grand old cathedrals was that they encouraged the petitioner to look up where she imagined God would be.

With her eyes turned toward gilded angels and ancient protectors, Sarah murmured her prayers. Then she went to a bank of glowing votives and lit two candles, one for love and one for healing. As she left the church and stepped into the sunshine it occurred to her that they were one and the same.

"How was your day?" Jim asked when they met back at the room.

"Great." Sarah pulled a top hat from her shopping bag. "Look. I found this for Dad. His other one is getting frayed."

"It makes me want to dance the old soft shoe."

Jim put it on his head, and danced around the room. At least, he tried to. He'd never been much of a dancer.

Sarah laughed and clapped, and that was enough reward for Jim. He was feeling good about the surprise he and Ben had cooked up for her, although it wasn't what he'd intended.

"You want what?" they'd shouted at him when he made his request. "Impractical. Impossible. Certainly not on this short notice."

So Jim had tucked that dream of Sarah's into his back pocket and gone on to plan B. He never stopped to question why he wanted to make her dreams come true. One look at her standing across the room with her eyes shining and her skin glowing was answer enough.

Jim tossed the top hat onto the dresser and held out his arms.

"Come here." Smiling, she moved into his arms, and he nuzzled his face against her hair. "I haven't seen you all day. It's been too long."

"Oh, Jim, for me, too."

She lifted her face to his and he started kissing her. *One quick kiss before dinner,* he promised himself. Just a taste to tide him over.

With Sarah, once was never enough. Moaning, he cupped her hips and pulled her closer, deepening the kiss. Desire came so quickly, an urgent hunger that heated his blood until he lost all reason.

Locked in each other's arms, they moved irrevocably toward the bed.

"I want to please you, Jim," Sarah whispered.

"You do. Always."

He could tell how pleased she was, and wished he could say more. He wished he could say, "You please me more than any woman I've known," but that would sound too much like a commitment.

As wonderful as she was, as intelligent, as sweet, as desirable, he couldn't possibly make promises. He didn't know what his own future held, let alone the future of someone else.

The thought made him unutterably sad, and when Sarah looked into his face, concerned and asking what was wrong, he told her nothing.

Then to show that he meant it he reached for her and began to kiss her again.

"Nothing you can't cure," he murmured.

Her sigh of contentment was his reward. She lifted herself on her elbows and traced his face with her fingertips.

"Jim, will you do something for me?"

"Anything within my power."

"Show me what you like. *Everything.*" She blushed. "Don't hold anything back."

Passion was a comet streaking through him, and as he began his instructions, he knew they'd never make it to dinner.

When Sarah woke up the sun was already shining through the French doors and Jim was nowhere to be seen. Alarmed, she threw back the covers and that's when she saw the makeshift diploma on his pillow. Sarah Sloan, Ph.D. in the Art of Love, the letters proclaimed.

She clutched it to her chest and laughed until tears rolled down her face.

"I'm glad you like it."

Jim appeared from the bathroom, wrapped in a towel.

"I never knew this much happiness was possible," she said. She was very close to declaring her love, then something in his face warned her not to go on. Jim looked dark and troubled.

*What's wrong?* was on the tip of her tongue, but the way he held himself so aloof and erect warned her against that, too.

"Today is Ben's graduation," he said, and Sarah's heart sank.

Today was their last day in New Orleans.

"I'd better get dressed," she said, then hurried from the room before he could see her tears.

Ben graduated at the top of his class. Sarah couldn't have been more thrilled if he had been her own brother, and she told him so. Wrapping her in a bear hug, he whispered, "Thanks, sis," then leaned back and winked at her as if the two of them had shared a great secret.

Sarah's heart broke a little. More than anything in the world she wanted what Ben said to be true: she wanted to have the right to be called his sister. The chances of that were not good, and getting worse every minute.

From the time they woke up this morning, she'd felt Jim pulling back. He'd acted the same. Or tried to. But she'd seen the same misgivings in his face that she felt in her heart. The same big question.

What would happen next with them?

The three of them spent the rest of the day together, walking and talking and laughing. Night came all too soon.

Her last night with Jim. Sarah felt the press of tears against her eyes, and she sought valiantly to hold them back.

"Close your eyes, Sarah, I have something for you," Jim said when they got back to the room, and for a thrilling moment she thought it might be a ring.

"Okay, you can open them now."

He was holding an enormous box. Much too big for a ring. Unless, of course, there was a series of smaller boxes inside.

*Funny,* Sarah thought, *how hope refuses to die.*

"Open it, Sarah."

She dawdled with the ribbon, stalled over the tape, dithered lifting the lid. The longer she waited, the longer her dream stayed alive.

Finally there was nothing else she could do to prolong seeing the contents without looking like a complete idiot. She lifted the lid, and there was the most spectacular dress she'd ever seen, a soft pink confection with a skirt like moonbeams and a scarf that would float from her bare shoulders like something worn by Isadora Duncan.

"It's beautiful," she said. And she meant it. She held it against her, and saw immediately that it was a dress made for dancing.

She might have protested that it was much too expensive a gift, that she didn't deserve it, that she had nothing with which to reciprocate. She might even have viewed it as a payoff for the five days, if she were that kind of woman.

But she wasn't. Thank goodness. She accepted his gift in the spirit he had offered. With grace and charm. She hoped.

"Will you wear it tonight, Sarah?"

"I wouldn't think of wearing anything else."

Ben picked them up at eight. He whistled when he saw Sarah.

"Hey, Jim, why don't you stay home tonight, then folks will think *I'm* with this gorgeous creature?"

"Charm runs in the Standing Bear family," Sarah said, but she was extraordinarily pleased.

Tomorrow she would leave this city behind, but she had tonight. She had Jim on one arm and his brother on the other, and she wasn't going to let anything stand in the way of enjoying her last hoorah in New Orleans.

Jim didn't tell her where they were going. Instead he kept saying, "Wait and see." Sarah could tell from his face how excited he was. Ben, too. They kept exchanging smug glances.

"What is this?" she said.

"You'll find out soon enough," Jim said. "It's a surprise."

When she heard the band, she knew. It was a swing band, playing the songs that made folks want to dance. Even before she saw it, she knew there was a dance floor inside, something covered with shiny parquet and high above, shimmering shiny balls sending showers of silver from the ceiling.

Her heart's rhythm increased and her palms felt dry.

"Here we are." Jim swept her into the room, and for a minute she thought he was going to say, "Ta Dah!" That's how pleased he looked.

Her heart climbed to her throat, and she thought she was going to faint. All the old memories swam to the surface, the old pain.

Sarah had not danced in public since her humiliation in New York. Dancing in the garden was different.

There was no one around to say, "Look how plain she is. She'll never make it. She should go home where she belongs."

Jim couldn't know, of course. And he never would.

"Do you like it, Sarah?" he asked, and she lied. She would tell a thousand lies to keep him from knowing how the sight of that dance floor terrified her.

"Yes." She even managed a smile. "It's a beautiful place, and the band is great."

He'd reserved a table near the dance floor. They ordered drinks, then sat talking and enjoying the band.

*Maybe that's enough,* she thought. *Just listening to the band.*

Jim leaned toward her when they played the "Tennessee Waltz."

"Sarah, I'm not much of a dancer, but I would love to have this dance with you."

She saw a vision of herself as an object of public ridicule. And then she saw Jim…really *saw* him.

His nobility was shining through. His courage. His steadfastness. Here was the man who had walked for her. How could she refuse to dance for him?

"It will be my pleasure."

Panicked and trying not to show it, she reached for his hand. She was going to make a fool of herself. She'd forgotten every dance step she ever knew.

He led her onto the dance floor and pulled her into his arms.

Sarah's feet remembered first, then her stiff arms, then her whole body, and quite suddenly she was dancing. *Really* dancing. Twirling around a polished floor in a public place with the man she loved.

She felt beautiful.

\* \* \*

Every mile the odometer ticked off was a stake driven through Jim's heart. He couldn't believe it was over.

He couldn't believe it had ever happened.

*Jim and Sarah and a love that made the world stand still.*

*No, not love,* he corrected himself. *Something else. Passion. That was it.*

He'd let himself get carried away by passion. The only way he could salve his conscience was by looking at Sarah. She positively glowed. Did that mean he hadn't done any harm? God, he hoped that was the case. He prayed it was.

She was quiet sitting on her side of the car. Every now and then she'd steal a glance at him and her cheeks would color up. Then she'd smile.

She had a beautiful smile. If he never remembered anything else about the past five days, he would remember Sarah's smile.

The sign on the side of the road said, Pensacola, ten miles. They were almost home.

What was he going to say to this trusting woman? *Thanks for the fun? See you around?*

He turned onto their street. Soon he'd be at their houses. That was it. They lived close enough to pop over every now and then and...

*And what, jerk? Have a quick tumble in the hay?*

Sarah was worth more than that. Far more. She deserved it all, the ring, the marriage, the husband. Things he couldn't give her. Things that required a man with a future.

"Well, here we are." He sounded like some sappy counselor welcoming reluctant children to summer camp. His skin was stretched tight over a smile that wouldn't pass for good humor in a thousand years.

"Thank you, Jim." Sarah offered her hand. "For everything."

*Saved by Sarah's grace.* Why didn't that make him feel better?

"It was my pleasure."

She was looking at him with bright expectancy, and his heart was doing funny things in his chest. He didn't want to tell her goodbye.

"Sarah."

"Yes?" She beamed him a look that broke his heart.

He cupped her face and kissed her on the lips, softly, tenderly. To take more would be unfair.

"Take care of yourself, Sarah Sloan." He caressed her face, memorizing every inch of it with his hands. "If you ever need anything, anything at all, call me."

"Yes, I will," she said, but he knew she wouldn't. She had too much pride.

He got her things and escorted her to the door. His footsteps sounded like bombs dropping on the pavement. Right up until the time he reached her door he was trying to think of a way they could recapture New Orleans, recreate it right here in Pensacola.

*Selfish bastard. Let it go.* Clean cuts healed quickly, didn't they?

She lingered in the doorway with a wistful look on her face that made him want to kiss her again. And again.

Why prolong the agony? Jim rammed his hands into his pockets. Hard.

"Well, then..." Her voice washed over him like silk, like the silk he'd stripped away from her last night right before they took that long, heady journey into the land of erotic pleasures.

Desire reared its insistent head right there on her doorstep, and need of her became an ache in his heart that might never go away.

"Bye, Jim."

She sounded like a little girl, lost, and the words he'd meant to say got clogged in his throat. Mumbling something he hoped passed for goodbye, he hurried across the porch and down the steps.

He didn't look back until he was safely in his house. And when he did he thought of Sarah dancing in his arms with her skirt swirling around her like moonbeams.

He wondered if she would ever dance again.

Julie was waiting for her, and the minute she saw Sarah's face she said, "What's wrong?"

"Nothing," Sarah said, trying to be brave, but all the bravado in the world couldn't cover the flood of misery that churned inside her.

Julie saw right through her. "Come into the kitchen and I'll make us some tea."

"Let me put my bags up."

"Forget the bags. They'll keep."

Julie busied herself with tea things while Sarah tried not to glance out the window to see if she could see anything at the house next door.

Guilt smote her. Here she was thinking of her own problems and she hadn't even asked about her father.

"How did it go with Dad?"

"Oh, Lord, Sarah. He's a handful. We've got to do something."

"Julie..." Her sister was working up to another awful discussion about a nursing home. "You know how I feel about that."

"Okay. All right." Julie threw up her hands. "I'm just glad you're back, that's all." Julie set the teacups on the table, then pulled out a chair. "Now, tell me what's wrong."

"I fell in love while I was in New Orleans, long before that, actually, and now he's gone and he's not ever coming back." Sarah put her hand over her heart. "I don't think I can breathe without him, Julie."

"It's Jim Standing Bear, isn't it?"

There was no use denying it. Obviously Julie had seen him drive off. Or maybe she'd put two and two together.

Sarah merely nodded. If she said more her dam of tears would burst and she might never stop crying.

"You're going to be all right, Sarah."

Her suave assurances made Sarah mad. "How do you know? How can you possibly know?"

"Do you know how many men I loved before I married George?" Julie didn't wait for an answer. Instead she held up three fingers. "I loved every one of them, but with each goodbye, I learned something.

"Now, you listen hard, Sarah. I learned that I am a strong and wonderful and worthy woman all by myself. I don't need anybody to validate that. And neither do you."

Suddenly Julie grinned. "You didn't know I was so wise, did you? Admit it."

"Well, of course, I've… No, I didn't."

"All right, then, truth time. Does he love you back?"

"I don't know."

"So what are you going to do? Sit over here and wallow in despair? No sirree, you are not. You're going over there tomorrow and have a heart-to-heart talk with him. I'll bet you didn't even tell him how you felt, did you?''

Sarah didn't have to say anything. Her expression was a dead giveaway.

"I knew it," Julie said. "You're going to march yourself over there tomorrow and tell him the truth. Promise me, Sarah."

Already, Sarah was feeling better. What if Jim was sitting in his kitchen just as miserable as she? What if he thought she didn't love him?

"I promise."

It was a promise she didn't keep. That night a tropical storm blew out of the gulf, smashed into Biloxi, Mississippi and spawned rain squalls as far east as Tallahassee. Sarah awoke to the sound of torrential rain slashing against her windows.

She rolled over and pulled the pillow over her head, but sleep wouldn't come. Something besides the rain was disturbing her, pricking at her until she finally got out of bed and tiptoed down the hall.

Her father's door was ajar. In the dim glow of the night-light she could see Evelyn Grimes asleep in her chair.

Alarm skittered through Sarah. Across the room her father's bed was empty.

"Mrs. Grimes, wake up." She shook the woman's shoulder. "Where's Dad?"

Evelyn Grimes sputtered and snorted, then sat bolt upright.

"He's right..." She looked at the empty bed, and guilt spread across her face. "I was feeling a little sick... I went to the bathroom... I must have closed my eyes for just a minute."

There was no telling how long the woman had been asleep, nor how long she'd been sleeping on the job, which could account for all the nights Sarah had found her father in the garden. But none of that was important now. What mattered was finding her father.

"You search the house. I'll look in the garden."

Sarah didn't even stop for her shoes. She took the stairs two at a time, and raced into the garden.

"Dad!"

Rain soaked her gown and plastered her hair to her head. It was coming down in thick sheets that beat the flowers to the ground and obscured the garden furniture. Sarah couldn't even see her garden angel.

"Dad," she called, panicked now, frantic, running through the garden like a madwoman, searching for the man she knew in her heart was not there.

She stumbled on the slick stone and went down onto her knees.

"Please, God," she prayed. "Please."

She struggled to her feet and covered every inch of the garden, searching for her dad and calling his name.

Jim sat straight up in bed, and he was saying, "Sarah." She'd disturbed his dreams all night. Was he still dreaming of her?

The storm beat against his house and the winds rattled the windowpanes. *Sarah.* Her name whispered through his mind once more and the hairs at the back of his neck stood on end.

Something was wrong. Jim felt it in his bones. He grabbed his pants and shirt. He wasn't about to ignore his instincts this time. The last time he'd done that he'd cracked himself to pieces on the bridge crossing the causeway.

He heard her the minute he stepped out his front door, or was that the wind? Jim sprinted toward the hedge.

*There.* The sound came again. It was definitely Sarah, calling for her father, and it was coming from the garden.

"Sarah! It's me. Jim."

She was on her knees, soaked and shaken. Jim scooped her up and held her close, consequences be damned.

"Tell me Sarah, what's wrong?"

"It's Dad." She was clutching a pair of sodden suede slippers. "These are his. Oh, Jim…"

Sobs shook her, and she buried her face against his chest.

"It's going to be all right, Sarah. We'll find him."

"How? He's not in the garden. I've looked everywhere."

"We *will* find him, Sarah. But first we have to get you out of that wet gown and into some clothes."

He hoped he sounded more confident than he felt. In this city somewhere was one lone old man who didn't even know his own name. Sending a prayer winging upward, he headed to the house.

Sarah had never been so glad to see anybody in her life. Jim would make everything all right. She pressed closer to him, inhaled his familiar scent. She was selfish. Selfish to the core. Stealing pleasure in the midst of her father's disappearance.

"I can walk, Jim."

Thankfully he ignored her. Her knees hurt, she was cold and wet, and she was so tired of being in charge she wanted to weep for the next eighteen Tuesdays.

"You've hurt yourself," he said, looking at the bloodstain on her gown.

"It's nothing. Just scraped my knees."

"Scraped knees don't qualify as *nothing,* Sarah."

Jim shoved open the door with his shoulder, and Mrs. Grimes met him in the hallway. Her severely plucked eyebrows shot up into her hairline when she saw Jim and Sarah.

"Did you find him?" Sarah asked.

She was surprised at how calm she sounded. It was mostly due to Jim. He was rock-hard and enduring. Being in his arms was like being in the protective lee of a mountain.

"No. I've looked everywhere."

"Then look again. Especially in the closets."

Mrs. Grimes disappeared into the library.

"Which way to your bedroom?" Jim asked.

"Upstairs."

He strode that way, still carrying her as if she were a newborn.

"What are you doing? Put me down. We've got to find Dad."

"I'm taking you upstairs so you can see about that knee and get out of those wet clothes. *I'll* find your father."

"Not without me, you won't."

They had reached her bedroom, and under other circumstances she'd have been giddy at the thought of the Bear standing among her personal things. The three-way mirror on her dressing table reflected the two of them, and the vision brought back so many memories, she wanted to cry.

Jim set her on a chair. "Don't move," he ordered, then he was in her bathroom, rummaging through the medicine cabinet. When he came back he had hydrogen peroxide, iodine ointment and bandages.

"Here. Take care of your knees, then put on some dry clothes. I'll be back before you know it."

"Wait a minute." Sarah scrambled for her shoes. "You're not going anywhere without me."

"Your knee is banged up, you're soaked to the skin—"

"I'm going, Jim. He's my dad."

For a moment he looked as if he would argue. Then he picked her up and carried her to the bed. Another time, another place whispered through the room, and their gazes met, held. A flame leaped in his eyes, and he bent so close she thought he was going to kiss her.

She *wanted* him to kiss her. Here. Now. She wanted it so much she almost cried out for it.

Shame came hard on the heels of desire. What kind of woman was she? If love made a person this selfish, she wanted nothing to do with it.

"Jim..." She licked lips suddenly gone dry.

He set her gently on the bed, then cupped her face. "If I leave you, you'll change clothes and ignore your knee."

His hand was on her gown, the silk sliding through his fingers. Sarah was not in her room at all. She was on a wrought-iron balcony, smelling the gardenias, feeling Jim's lips against her own.

"I'm just going to take care of your knee, Sarah," he murmured. "That's all."

"Hurry, Jim. Every second we lose is precious."

"This will only take a second... There. See. Now get into some dry clothes. I'll wait for you downstairs."

He left her bedroom, and Sarah took a long shuddering breath. Then she grabbed jeans and a sweater, rammed her feet into loafers without socks. Jim was waiting for her downstairs.

"I spoke with the police. They're going to patrol the area, and I talked with Mrs. Grimes again. He's definitely not in the house. Have you any idea where he might have gone?"

"None."

"Come on, then. Let's get going. Where's your raincoat?"

Sarah reached into the closet to nab a slicker, and Jim covered her hand.

"Don't worry, Sarah. He can't have gone far. We'll find him. I promise you."

It was a promise she *had* to believe.

"Jim…thank you for being here," she said, and then they walked out into the dark streets to begin their search.

## Chapter Fifteen

They'd searched for hours, walking from neighborhood to neighborhood, hoping to turn up a clue. There was nothing. Her dad had completely vanished.

"You're tired, Sarah. I'm calling a cab for you."

She was so weary and footsore she thought she might never walk anywhere again as long as she lived. Even if she only wanted to go two blocks, she would take a cab.

Jim pulled out his cellular phone, but she put a hand over his.

"No. We have to find him, Jim."

"You're soaked."

It was true. Even with the slicker, she was wringing wet. Rain had found its way through every possible opening. Her shoes squished when she walked, her hair was drenched, and her clothes soggy.

"It doesn't matter. Nothing matters except finding Dad."

"It will be light soon, Sarah. I can get some helicopters from the base to search."

"That sounds so ominous, Jim. So hopeless."

Weren't helicopter searches a last resort? She was afraid to ask. They were coming up to a major thoroughfare, four lanes filled with predawn traffic. On the corner stood a telephone booth and a ubiquitous concrete bench.

"Let's sit here and regroup," Jim said, and Sarah slumped gratefully onto the hard cold seat.

He draped an arm lightly around her shoulders. She would have given everything she owned to snuggle into him and put her head on his shoulder and cry. But she had too much pride.

What was more, he'd make it perfectly clear that he didn't want her in that way any more. Or had he?

She stared at the flow of traffic while Jim called police headquarters to see if they'd turned up anything. She didn't have to ask. His face said it all.

"I'm sorry, Sarah."

She squinted up at the streetlights while fat hot tears rolled down her cheeks. She hoped Jim would think it was rain.

"I'll call Julie as soon as it's light," she said.

"We're at the end of the residential section. Maybe we'll turn up something on the way back home."

"Maybe," she said, but she didn't really believe it.

Long ago on a crowded backstage in New York she'd learned the folly of being an eternal optimist. And even though Jim had given her back a part of her dream, she was still realistic enough to know that their chances of finding her father grew slimmer with every hour that passed.

"Let's go back, Jim."

She turned her collar up against the rain, for all the good it did, and was turning around when something across the street caught her eye. A green umbrella with purple pansies. Julie's umbrella. The one she'd left behind yesterday.

"Jim, wait." She clutched his sleeve.

"What is it, Sarah?"

"Across the street..."

The umbrella emerged from the crowd, and underneath was her dad, dressed in striped pajamas, dancing barefoot through the rain.

"It's Dad!"

The words were no sooner out of her mouth than her father danced toward the curb and twirled onto the highway. A biker swerved to miss him and almost lost control of his motorcycle on the slick highway.

Oblivious, Dr. Eric Sloan kept on dancing.

"Oh, my God, he's going to get killed," she said, but Jim didn't hear.

He was already racing across the street, dodging traffic. Brakes squealed. Drivers rolled down their windows and swore.

They were both going to be killed. Sarah couldn't bear to watch...and she couldn't bear not to. Jim had made it across three lanes, but a city garbage truck was bearing down on him.

Would the driver see the two people over the hood of his elevated truck? Even if he did, could he stop in time?

Sarah covered her mouth with her hands to stop the

scream. The driver didn't see them. He never checked his speed.

"Fred, go back!" Jim yelled. "Go back to the curb!"

Her father smiled and waved and kept on dancing.

Sarah died a thousand deaths. The two people she cared about most in the world were going to be killed. Or maimed for life.

"No," she whispered. "Not Jim. Please, God, not Jim. Not again."

He was walking because of one miracle. Was it too much to ask for two? Was it selfish to ask for more than your share?

Sarah didn't care. The garbage truck bore down on Jim, and she prayed as she never had in her life.

Everything seemed to happen in slow motion. Jim running and running, his hitched gait glaringly obvious. Her father tap dancing and singing in the rain, blissfully unaware of danger, waving to his audience. Cars pulling over to the curb, brakes squealing. A crowd gathering across the street, some of them screaming. The garbage truck, barreling toward tragedy.

It was only a few feet away from Jim and her dad. Jim made a flying tackle and the truck roared by. Sarah cried.

"Jim! Dad!"

What was happening? She couldn't see. She didn't know.

Sarah dodged across the street. "Let me through. Oh, please let me through. That's my father."

*And the man I love.* The words seared into her brain with absolute certainty. No matter what had happened, no matter what happened in the future, she loved Jim Standing Bear.

Oh, God, where was he? Where was Jim?

Traffic had come to a complete standstill. The garbage truck had stopped halfway down the block, and the driver was running back toward the crowd huddled around two fallen figures.

"Jim!" Sarah screamed.

And then, miraculously he was up, standing tall and proud, head and shoulders above the crowd.

"Sarah, it's okay. Your dad is okay."

He pushed his way through then wrapped a protective arm around her shoulders and led her toward the spot where a middle-aged man was bending over her dad.

"I thought you'd been killed," she said.

"We made it. It was nip and tuck for a while, but we both made it, Sarah."

At their approach, the crowd parted. Someone snapped pictures.

"Sarah, this is Glen Arnold, an off-duty fireman," he said, introducing her to the man who was examining her father.

"He's one very lucky man," Glen said. "He's going to be sore, but I don't think anything is broken."

Dr. Eric Sloan snorted. "The humorous is definitely broken, the scapula is probably fractured, and the femur hurts like hell. Thank God, it's not broken, otherwise I'd be out of a career."

Smiling he offered his hand. "I'm Fred Astaire, young man, an American institution in case you didn't know, and I don't know who that fellow is standing over there with Ginger, but he sure ruined my act."

Laughing and crying at the same time, Sarah bent over her father.

"That man is Lieutenant Commander Jim Standing Bear, and he saved your life."

"Next time, Commander, wait till the show is over."

Her father looked fragile lying in the hospital bed with his arm in a cast and bruises on his face. Fragile and so very needy.

Now that it was all over, Sarah couldn't seem to stop shaking. She set aside the coffee someone had brought her. The nurse? Julie? Jim?

He was nowhere to be seen. He'd been with her every step of the way—during the all-night search, on the long ride in the ambulance, during the agonizing wait while doctors examined her father.

He'd been the one to call Julie, the one to tell Julie and George about the disappearance and subsequent search. He'd taken care of a hundred small details while Sarah leaned against the wall and quietly fell apart.

"Are you okay?" Julie wrapped her arm around Sarah.

"Yes. I will be. Where's Jim?"

"He left a little while ago. He said to tell you he'd see you later."

"Did he see a doctor? Somebody should examine him. Where was I and why didn't somebody come and get me?"

"Whoa." Julie studied her with lips pursed and eyes squinted. "Breathe."

"I didn't even thank him," she said, and then she started to cry.

"Here." Julie motioned for George to stand watch while she led her sister into the waiting room. "Go ahead and cry. Lord knows, you deserve it."

"I do not deserve it. Dad's the one who's been hurt. And Jim." She pressed her hands over the sledgehammers that were pounding her temples. "When I think how close he came to getting hit, he and Dad both…"

"They didn't. That's the main thing. What we have to do now is decide what we're going to do."

"Going to do? About what?'

"Dad. Now don't get your dander up. You can't keep on like this, Sarah."

"I'm going to fire Mrs. Grimes and hire another night sitter."

"Dad will only keep finding ways to run away. It's part of the illness, Sarah." Julie went to the vending machine and came back with two Almond Joys. She handed one to Sarah. "Don't look so shocked. Do you think I don't read, too?"

"I didn't say that."

"I swear, Sarah. You're so busy taking care of the world you forget that there are other people who know a thing or two. Namely me."

Julie chomped down on her candy. Mad. Sarah knew it was delayed reaction to stress. Still, she felt guilty.

"I should have called you, Julie. I'm sorry."

"Yes. You should have. I should have been out in the dark, too, searching."

Sarah gave her a rueful smile. "I'll call you next time."

"There's not gong to be a next time. We're going to find a good secure place for Dad."

The thought of her dad being bundled up and sent

away broke Sarah's heart. Something inside her clenched and bowed up for a fight.

"I don't want Dad in a nursing home, Julie. How many times do I have to say it? I can take care of him myself."

"What are you going to do, Sarah? Stay on guard twenty-four hours a day?"

"Let's not talk about it now, Julie. I'm tired."

Too tired to fight. She'd save that for later. She would march through hell before she'd see her dad cared for by strangers.

Sarah had used Jim's title when she'd told her father who he was. Without it, who was he? A broken-down has-been, that's who. Even kindhearted, generous-spirited Sarah couldn't see him as separate from his career as an aviator with the U.S. Navy.

Jim poured himself another cup of coffee. He should have been exhausted from his night's work, but he wasn't. He should have been sleepy. Instead he was exhilarated, pumped-up, ready to go out and slay dragons.

Or at least to tackle his future.

It was time to make some decisions. Past time. Not only for himself, but for Sarah. She was the burr under his saddle, the carrot to his jackass.

He wanted to see her again. Not as a friend. Not as neighbor. He wanted to see her the way he had in New Orleans. As a lover. As a man with a future, a man who had the right to come courting.

He smiled at the old-fashioned terminology. Sarah deserved an old-fashioned courtship, one with pink roses to match her skin and chocolates filled with exotic fruit and nuts and moonlit nights filled with dancing.

He wanted to dance with her once more, to kiss her, to hold her.

Seeing her tonight and knowing he had no right to offer her more than friendship had been agony. The next time he saw her, he would offer her...

He wasn't sure what he'd offer. He wasn't even sure what his feelings were. His only certainty was that his feelings for Sarah Sloan were intense, bordering on obsessive.

He drank his third cup of coffee, then went upstairs to shave and change clothes. Sarah would have to wait. The first thing on his agenda was a visit to the Pensacola Naval Air Station.

The roar of jets. The mushrooming contrails. The sleek aircraft. The spit and polish of dress blues.

All of it overwhelmed Jim. He stood beside his car in the parking lot of the air base shaking so badly he didn't think he could stand, let along go inside.

Two Hornets streaked across the sky, flying so close it looked as if their wings were touching. A couple of Blue Angels, taking a trial spin.

The ache inside Jim was as big as the Grand Canyon. Bigger. He was falling into his hurt, and soon he would vanish. He fought against the pain, wrestled with loss, struggled against defeat.

The victory was hard-fought and slow in coming, but he won. Finally, he won.

With the military bearing of a man who was proud to be in the service of his country, Lieutenant Commander Jim Standing Bear went inside.

Commander Chuck Sayers was more than Jim's superior officer; he was his friend. A huge grin split his face when Jim walked into his office.

"Bear!" Chuck embraced him, then pounded him on the back. "Good lord, you're a sight for sore eyes. Sit down, tell me what's happening, how've you been?"

"Lower than a toad and meaner than a grizzly."

"Ben told us you weren't seeing anybody."

"I couldn't. Too many reminders. I hope there are no hard feelings, Chuck."

"I understand. Hell, I can say that, and it sounds so artificial. You're back, Bear. That's all that matters."

Chuck picked up a pen and twirled it between his fingers, a sure sign he was nervous.

"You *are* back, aren't you? You're not thinking of doing anything foolish like resigning your commission or taking a disability discharge, are you?"

"The thought had crossed my mind." At Chuck's look of alarm, Jim added, "Briefly."

"Thank God."

The two old friends and flying buddies studied each other, aware that their relationship was now different and uncertain how to handle the change.

*Get it out in the open,* Jim told himself.

"I saw a couple of Hornets when I drove in. Who's flying my position now?"

"Lt. Everett Haske is flying right wing now, Bear. He's a good kid. A Californian. Got his gold wings in '91. He's not you, but he's trying really hard, and I think he's eventually going to be an asset to the team."

Chuck spun his pen round and round. "I'm damned sorry, Bear."

"What's done is done. It's useless to look back. I should know. I did it for six months."

"Ben told me that you were walking."

"What else did Ben tell you?"

"He said that if you ever got your butt over here I should pin you to the wall until you agreed to stay."

Jim laughed. "Are you going to?"

"Do I have to?"

"No. I'm back, Chuck. To stay."

The pen spun across the desk once more, then Chuck gave Jim a squinty-eyed look.

"There's an opening for flight instructor."

*Grounded. Never to feel the power of the Hornet again. Never to fly so high and so fast he felt as if he'd touched the face of God.*

*Don't think of the things you've lost,* he told himself. *Think of the things you'll gain.*

Excellent flight training could mean the difference between life and death to a pilot. Jim *could* make a difference—for somebody else.

"I was hoping so," he said quietly.

After Sarah came home from the hospital, she fell into bed and slept like the dead for two hours. When she woke up she was alone in an empty house. Completely alone.

And it was all her fault. If she'd been vigilant her father wouldn't have run away. If she'd been paying attention to her family instead of running wild because of her heart, her dad would be donning an old top hat and yelling, "Let's dance, Ginger."

"Let's dance, Sarah," he used to say when she was six and full of ballerina dreams. He had given her the dreams, and so much more.

And she had repaid him by letting him down. "A nursing home," Julie had said.

"Over my dead body," Sarah muttered.

She saw herself in the full-length mirror as she headed for her bath. Where was the plain, gawky woman she'd been? It astonished Sarah now that she'd let a chance remark heard backstage become her Waterloo. Somebody had called her homely, and for years she'd worn the label like a scarlet letter instead of fighting back.

It had taken Jim to make her see herself as beautiful. The handsome Bear. The man who had turned her inside out, who had turned her world upside down.

The man she could never have. A pain caught her in the heart and wouldn't let go. Sarah turned on the water full force, but it didn't help. Every precious moment she'd spent with Jim played through her mind.

She couldn't say the exact moment she'd started loving him, for it felt as if she always had. This much she knew: she always would.

She counted herself lucky. Who would have imagined that a woman as plain as Sarah Sloan would have a romance, however brief, with a man as glorious as Jim Standing Bear? She had enough memories to last a lifetime.

And they had to. Her father had devoted his life to her and her sister. And now she would devote hers to him. Exclusively. There would be no repeats of what had happened last night.

A vision of Jim rose in her mind. *Paradise lost.*

"I won't think of him right now," she whispered. She couldn't afford to. She needed all her energy for the tasks ahead, facing down Julie and caring for her dad.

And she was going to fight Julie, no matter what the argument. Though her sister had the most loving intentions, she did tend to be bossy. And Sarah, the peacemaker, rarely argued.

Well, she was through being the complacent sister. From now on she was Sarah the warrior. Not warrior princess. That was too fussy and prissy. Sarah Sloan was a warrior. A woman to be reckoned with.

And God help the first person who crossed her.

She was still in the tub when the doorbell rang. Julie, probably. She wrapped herself in her robe, and went downstairs barefoot.

"Coming," she said when the doorbell pinged again. "Just a minute, Julie."

"Sorry to disappoint you."

It was Jim Standing Bear on her front porch, and all Sarah's newfound courage went out the window.

The sight of Sarah fresh from her bath dealt Jim a blow he hadn't expected. He had come to ask about her father. Or so he'd thought. He'd come to tell her that he was no longer a man adrift. Or so he'd believed.

But Sarah's hair was slicked back and her skin was dew-damp and her eyes were shining, and all he could think about was kissing her.

Fortunately, she was just as discomfited as he. The best plan would be a quick inquiry, then a hasty retreat.

"I've come at a bad time," he said. "I can come back."

"No. Come in." He noticed how she tightened her belt as if she were girding herself for battle. Or perhaps she thought he might rip it from her body. Which was exactly what he wanted to do. Maybe not rip. Peel. That was it. He wanted to peel the robe away slowly so that she was offered up to him bit by enticing bit.

"I should have called first," he said.

"Actually, I'm glad you came. It gives me a chance to thank you for all you've done for me and my family."

"You're more than welcome, Sarah."

There was something different about her, something Jim couldn't put his finger on, something exciting and slightly dangerous. Not that she hadn't always been exciting. Still, she had a new edge that took his breath away. And nearly took his control.

He wrested it back. *One step at a time,* he reminded himself. Now was the time to support her, not court her.

"There's something I've been wanting to know," she said. "How did you know something was wrong?"

Was it only last night? It seemed like a million years.

"Intuition, Sarah. Every pilot has it to a certain degree. I've been gifted with more than my share. It's almost a clairvoyance." He smiled at her. "Ben claims it's all part of the Native American heritage, and that's quite an admission coming from somebody who has to see it under a microscope to believe it."

Jim couldn't believe himself. He sounded like a damned magpie. Ben would laugh his head off if he could hear.

"How is your father?" He wished he had asked the question first.

"He's going to be fine, thanks to you."

"I'm sorry I had to leave the hospital without saying goodbye. There was something I had to do. Something important."

Now what? Sarah was as polite as usual, but her usual avid interest was missing. Jim blundered on.

"I went to see Commander Chuck Sayers, Sarah. At the base. I'm going back, as flight instructor."

"I'm glad, Jim."

Her smile was genuine. But her interest was still tepid. What had he expected? That she'd jump through hoops? She had a father in the hospital, worries on her mind.

Feeling awkward and just a bit foolish, Jim stood up. If he'd had on a hat he would be twisting it in his hands.

"You'll let me know if there's anything I can do. Anytime, Sarah. Day or night."

A faint blush crept into her cheeks.

*So, she's not as unmoved as she seems.* Jim indulged in a bit of selfish glee. Pride, he guessed. He wanted Sarah to desire him as much as he desired her.

"Thank you, Jim."

Except for the telltale blush, her face gave nothing away. There was nothing left to say, nothing left to do except leave.

"I can see myself out. Goodbye, Sarah."

Her goodbye was so soft he barely heard her. He was still reeling from the encounter when he got home.

He made himself a spartan dinner, then went up to his rooftop. To watch the stars.

Jim adjusted his telescope, then shoved it aside in disgust. He hadn't come to watch stars; he'd come to watch Sarah's garden. In case she came. In case she danced.

* * *

Sarah didn't know how long she sat in her chair not moving after Jim left. It was the only way she could keep from breaking apart.

Eventually she went upstairs to her bedroom. She took the dance dress out of her closet, folded it and wrapped it in tissue paper. Then she took the make-shift diploma from her bedside table and placed it on top of the dress.

Walking as if the floor were mined, Sarah went to the attic and placed the items in an old steamer trunk.

She wouldn't be needing them anymore.

If Jim had not been back on active duty, he'd have hung around the telephone waiting for Sarah to call. As it was, he only haunted his phone during the night-time hours. That and the rooftop.

But the phone was silent, the garden, empty.

Sarah had her first confrontation with her sister the day her father came home from the hospital. She could tell by the way Julie's jaw was set that a storm was brewing.

*Please, God,* Sarah prayed. *Not till after we get him home.*

She got her wish, but as soon as their father was settled upstairs, Julie cornered her.

"We have to talk, Sarah."

"Not now, Julie. I have to take Dad's medicine upstairs."

She escaped for a while, Sarah the Scared, hiding from her sister. Whatever had happened to Sarah the Warrior?

"I don't like these things." Her father took the pills out of his mouth. "They make me sleepy."

"You have to have them." Sarah gently moved them back into his mouth.

"I could spit them out as soon as you leave, you know." He gave her a devilish grin. "I just might, you know."

"Please. Swallow them. For me."

"Mail me a letter," he said.

This sort of rambling was not new. The sad part was that it was getting worse.

"All right. If you'll take the pills, I'll mail you a letter."

He swallowed his medicine, then began to pick at the covers.

"The letter needs stamps. I didn't have any stamps."

"Don't worry. I'll get you some." She smoothed the covers, then kissed his parchmentlike cheek. "Rest now."

It was what Jim had said to her in New Orleans. Sarah's knees and resolve both weakened. She leaned her head against the bedpost and closed her eyes, then she went downstairs to face her sister.

## Chapter Sixteen

When Jim came home from the base, he found Delta in the kitchen polishing silver and muttering to herself.

"The house looks great, Delta."

"Humph."

"Does that mean I should get out of the kitchen and not make myself a well-deserved cup of tea until after you've gone?"

"It's all the same to me."

Jim filled the teapot and got out the teabags.

"How's Sarah?"

He hoped he sounded friendly but casual. It had been three days since he'd seen her, three of the longest days of his life.

"That poor child is running herself ragged. Savannah says the new night sitter is not worth a toot, and it don't help none that you're sitting over here like a lump on a log."

"I told her to call me anytime she needed help."

"Humph. I reckon when your legs started working your brain went on strike."

"What's that supposed to mean?"

"Them's easy words to say, Jim, but helping ain't in the offerin', it's in the doin'. How many folks you know ever pick up the phone and say, 'I need some help over here?' Nobody, that's who."

She was right, of course. Although offers of that kind were sincerely given, most people didn't respond. Sometimes it was a simple matter of pride. Sometimes guilt was the motive. Caregivers were especially prone to that one.

At this very moment, Sarah was probably eaten up with guilt, imagining herself the cause of her father's problems.

Delta left off her silver polishing to pat Jim on the cheeks.

"Both of you's my babies, and both of you's hurtin'."

Then Delta, who could go from outraged to charming in the space of a heartbeat, gave him a big smile that showed her gold teeth.

"The Bear I know is fixin' to do something about it."

"What can I do, Delta?"

"I'm sure you'll think of something."

He spent the rest of the evening doing just that. What could he give Sarah that she didn't already have? Delta did the housework, Savannah did the daytime sitting, Jared mowed her yard.

Her house and grounds were being cared for. But what about her soul? What about her heart?

He wanted to do something to bring back the glow

she'd had in New Orleans, the spontaneous laughter, the sense of joy. Given the mood she'd been in when he last saw her, she probably wouldn't leave the house to have a meal, much less anything else.

For a while Jim got caught up in *anything else,* and he could do nothing but stare out the window and long. Under the present circumstances, recreating what they'd had in New Orleans was impossible.

Besides, there was no such thing as going back. All he could do was go forward. Where that forward momentum would take him, he didn't know. All he knew was that he had to start moving.

Sarah used to love going to the grocery store. She enjoyed browsing among the produce, thumping the melons and hefting the Indian River grapefruit and admiring the strawberries. If she didn't have a schedule to keep, she would spend as much as two hours prowling the aisles and happily contemplating what she would do with the fresh peaches and what kind of sauce she would make for the orange roughy and whether to buy sorbet or ice cream to top the fruit pie she planned to make.

Nowadays she was always in a hurry. Sure, Savannah was with her dad, and Delta was taking care of the house, but what if he needed her?

What if he called for her and she wasn't there? Lately he'd been displaying a few of the aggressive tendencies the doctors had warned them about. When Lola Fisk, the new night sitter, had tried to take his new top hat off so he could go to bed, he'd swung at her. She threatened to quit and it took Sarah half an hour to convince her to stay.

She got huffy when Sarah wasn't there to greet her

in the evening when she came on shift. She had a way of pursing her lips so that her whole mouth looked zipped shut.

"How can I care for your father if I don't get a full report before I go on duty?" she would say.

And since their last fight over the nursing home, Julie was barely talking to her. Her silence made her position loud and clear.

"If you insist on being a martyr, don't expect me to make it easier for you."

It was getting harder and harder for Sarah to turn the negatives into positives. Mostly, she wanted to crawl into a cave and hibernate like the bears.

*Bear.* A pain hit her high up under the ribs, and she had to lean on her grocery cart until it went away.

She grabbed a cereal box and threw it into the cart without even checking the list of nutrients. What did nutrients matter when your heart was broken?

By the time she got home, her feet were dragging. Delta met her at the car to help bring in the bags.

Wonderful smells filled the kitchen. She so rarely had time to cook a real meal these days that she'd forgotten how good a house can smell at dinnertime.

Delta was standing by the refrigerator unloading lemons and oranges and grinning like the cat that swallowed the canary. Cooking was not part of her duties, though she did occasionally surprise Sarah with a batch of fried chicken or a crusty peach cobbler. Especially lately.

"It smells delicious in here." She hugged her housekeeper. "Thank you, Delta."

"You huggin' the wrong one."

"Savannah cooked?"

"Nah. The cook's out yonder in the backyard. You

might want to comb your hair before you go out there to thank him.''

Sarah raced to the window, and there in her back-yard was Jim Standing Bear swathed in a blue apron and wielding barbecue tools over the grill. Tears clogged her throat, and she put her hand over it to hold them in.

''Oh, my...''

''Well, don't just stand there gawkin', honey. Do something.''

Sarah headed toward the stairs then stopped in mid-flight. What did appearance matter when the man she loved was waiting in her backyard?

Reversing direction, she hurried to the back door, pausing only long enough to catch her breath before she went outside.

If he lived to be a hundred and ten, Jim would never forget the look on Sarah's face when she saw him turning a slab of ribs on her grill. That one look made it all worthwhile—the planning, the plotting with Delta and Savannah, the anxiety.

Until she stepped into the backyard, he'd questioned himself a hundred times over whether he was doing the right thing.

''I thought you and your dad might enjoy a back-yard barbecue,'' he said. ''I hope you don't mind.''

''Mind? I think it's wonderful.''

*You're the most wonderful man in the world.* Once she'd said that to him. Would she ever say it again?

She'd paused beside the chaise longue, and now she gripped the back of it as if she needed something to anchor her to the ground. At least, he hoped that's why she needed it.

From the minute she'd appeared, Jim felt a lurching

within himself as if he were getting ready to take flight.

"I hope you like barbecue."

"I love it."

Their eyes spoke a thousand things they couldn't say, and neither of them could look away. Jim stood with his barbecue fork poised in the air and Sarah stood gripping the chair.

Suddenly Jim had a vision of how things could be—small simple moments of joy mixed with heady pleasures that made the heart stand still. He imagined quiet comings and goings, soft kisses in the night, two tangled in the sheets while rain fell on the roof. Children.

His mind stalled. This was territory he wasn't ready to explore.

"Dinner will be ready in about fifteen minutes," he said, instead, and the hushed moment they'd shared vanished.

"I'll go upstairs and get Dad."

"I've made enough for Delta and Savannah, too."

"Good." She smiled. "You're very thoughtful, Jim."

It wasn't the high praise he'd basked in during their idyll in New Orleans, but it would do. For the moment, it would do.

Sarah raced upstairs and made a detour by her bathroom. Who was that flushed woman in the mirror? She put her hands over her hot cheeks, then bent over and dashed water on her face.

She couldn't afford to be excited. She couldn't let herself take one sweet moment and build it into a lifetime. Her life's course was already set.

She dried her face, reached for her lipstick, then

withdrew her hand. She didn't want Jim to think she'd primped for him. She didn't want him thinking anything except that she was grateful for his kindness.

Did she?

Dreams of what might have been washed over her. Weak-kneed, Sarah leaned against the sink and closed her eyes.

"I must not think of it," she said, but a vision of Jim bending over her with the early morning light shining on his face made her feel faint.

She sat down on the edge of the tub until she could pull herself together. Then she went to get her father.

Dr. Sloan wore his top hat. Not to be outdone, Savannah wore a gypsy skirt and gold dancing shoes. Delta was in her usual rainbow-colored garb.

Jim couldn't have been more pleased. All in all, dinner had a festive air. Savannah knew more funny stories than most stand-up comics, and she kept them all laughing throughout the meal.

Jim kept watching Sarah. As the meal progressed she began to relax, and by the time they got to dessert she had lost the anxious look she'd worn when she brought her father outside.

"This pie is delicious," Delta said, baiting him. "You ought to open a bakery."

"I already did, Delta. I opened the bakery door, went inside and asked for two lemon cream pies."

Everybody laughed, then Dr. Sloan said, "Did you get my letter, Commander?"

Jim didn't know how to reply. Fortunately, Sarah saved him.

"Yes, Fred, he got it."

Dr. Eric Sloan looked pleased, then the smile slid from his face and confusion took its place.

"I put it..." He glanced from Delta to Savannah, searching for answers, then his gaze settled on his daughter.

"Sarah?"

She knelt beside her father's chair and held his hand.

"Yes, Dad. It's me."

"The yard is full of people."

"They're our friends."

His lips trembled as he studied the friends whose names he didn't know.

"We'll go, Sarah," Jim said quietly. Savannah and Delta were already making their way into the kitchen.

"Thank you, Jim. For everything."

As he neared the back door he heard Dr. Sloan say, "Did you get my letter, Sarah?"

To have her father back, even for a few minutes, was a precious thing for Sarah. She didn't want to discuss a letter. Imaginary or otherwise. She wanted to say the important things.

"Don't worry about the letter, Dad. Just know that I love you and I'm going to take care of you."

"No. The letter, Sarah, you must read the letter."

He was getting agitated, and she sought to calm him.

"All right. I'll read it."

"Promise me!"

"I promise, Dad. Just tell me where it is."

"It's... I put it..." Tears stood in his eyes. "I don't remember."

She wrapped her arms around him. "It's all right, Daddy. I love you." She took off his top hat and smoothed his hair. "I love you, Daddy."

## Chapter Seventeen

When he looked at the eager young men sitting in his classroom Jim felt an emptiness that no amount of pleasure in teaching could fill. He'd lost the thing they looked forward to, flying.

He always left the base quickly when he got off duty, never looking up, never glancing toward the hangar. The sooner he was gone, the sooner he'd be away from the jets that roared through the sky.

Without him.

He gripped the steering wheel so hard his knuckles turned white. Scenery passed by unnoticed, and suddenly Jim found himself veering left instead of the right turn that would take him home.

The private airstrip was on Highway 97 north of Molino, and a twin-engine Baron sat in front of the hangar. A sign at the gate said Grover's Flight School and underneath it another said For Sale.

Chuck had mentioned the sale to Jim at lunch the day before, then he'd said, "Why don't you check it out, Jim?"

"Why would I want to check it out?" Jim asked, but he knew why. Pilots live for flight, and grounded ones carry a misery inside that nothing can abate. Chuck wanted to get him in the air again.

While the injuries Jim had sustained made it impossible to ever fly the Hornet again, flying a twin-engine plane was a different story. But flying a twin-engine plane couldn't compare with the thrill of flying a jet. Chuck knew that as well as Jim.

"Just a suggestion, that's all." Chuck had dropped the subject, but it had stayed in Jim's mind fermenting till it reached the point of explosion, he guessed. Or else why was he here?

Jim drove through the gates, then sat in his car wondering what crazy impulse had driven him there. Compared to the Hornet, the Baron looked a toy.

"What am I doing here?" he muttered.

He'd started his engine when a bowlegged man wearing aviator's glasses came out of the hangar wiping his hands on a chamois cloth.

"If you're wanting lessons..." His voice trailed off when he got closer. "You're the Bear, aren't you?" He gave a wry smile, then held out his hand. "I saw you in a show two years ago. Pleasure to meet you. I'm Grover."

Jim got out of his car and shook the man's hand.

"What can I do for you today, Lieutenant Commander?"

"I'd like to take the Baron up, if you don't mind. See how she flies."

The words had popped out of nowhere, and as Jim

approached the plane excitement sizzled through him. He could fly again. He *would*.

"The old girl would consider it a privilege, and so would I."

The minute he climbed into the cockpit, Jim knew he'd been right to come. As he taxied down the runway, the empty space inside him began to fill. He pulled back on the throttle, lifting the nose, climbing until he was in the skies once more.

He wasn't merely in them: he owned them. He had transcended the earth and he owned the heavens.

His heart was full to bursting. He was flying again, and nothing was impossible to him. Nothing. Not even love.

"Sarah," he whispered, breathing her name like a promise.

Sarah turned the house upside down looking for her father's letter. His stint into reality had been short-lived. It hadn't even lasted until she could get him back up the stairs after the barbecue—Jim's wonderful surprise.

Her cheeks flushed and her eyes misted over. *Don't think about Jim,* she told herself. If she did she would lose focus or go crazy or both.

She'd already searched the desk in her father's room as well as the desk inside the library, the drawers of the hall table, all the kitchen cabinets, the closet shelves.

Where else was there to look? Maybe she'd missed something the first time around. She was in the library going through the desk again when the doorbell rang.

Maybe Savannah would get it. Then she realized Savannah couldn't get the door: Sarah had given her a well-deserved day off. And it wasn't Delta's day to work.

Sighing, Sarah went to answer the door, then almost had a heart attack.

"Jim…" She pushed her hair back from a face suddenly gone hot.

"Hello, Sarah."

The way he said it sent shivers down her spine. The way he smiled melted her all the way down to her toes. The way he looked at her…

Sarah caught a sharp breath. The look he gave her was both predatory and possessive. Memories flooded her until she was drowning. She'd already gone under three times and soon she would be lost.

*Don't think about New Orleans. Don't think about the way he's looking at you.*

She couldn't help herself. His eyes blazed through her like comets, and her whole body was on fire. She guessed she'd have stood in the doorway forever if he hadn't said something.

"May I come in?"

"Forgive my bad manners. It's Delta's day off and Savannah's not here and I guess I'm flustered…with all there is to do," she added late, much, much too late.

Of course he'd know she was flustered by him. Who could help but see? She led him into the den.

"Can I get you something?"

"Yes." His smile dazzled her. "You."

"Ohh…"

Her hand flew to her chest to hold in her flyaway heart. It was beating like a caged bird straining to be free. Sarah meant to sit on the sofa like a lady, but her limp body betrayed her. She sort of slumped and slithered instead.

Her hem got stuck between the crushed velvet cushions. With her dress hiked over her knees and her heart pounding wildly, she sat there like a mannequin. Speechless.

Jim went down on one knee and took her hand. Sarah forgot to breathe.

"I'm asking you to marry me, Sarah."

Joy ricocheted through her, and hard on its heels, pain. She squeezed her eyes tightly together as if she could shut out the truth, the unbearable, horrible truth.

He turned her hands over and planted sweet hot kisses in her palms. The kisses seared her heart.

"Sarah, open you eyes."

How could she help but obey? She would do anything for Jim, anything except this.

"Will you marry me?"

"Oh, Jim…"

"I hope that's a *yes*. Say yes, Sarah."

The pain moved all over her, settling in her temples. Sledgehammers pounded them, and she thought she might faint.

"Sarah?" Jim slid onto the sofa and pulled her into his arms. "What's wrong?"

She thought of saying nothing. She considered dismissing his question with a light reply. In the end she could do neither. Jim had given her so much. He'd given her the world. Didn't he deserve the truth?

"Everything, Jim. Everything's wrong."

"Tell me and maybe I can make it right. I want to help you, Sarah."

He smoothed her hair, then kissed her softly on the lips. She leaned against him, savoring the feel of a solid wall of muscle, basking in the feeling of being protected, even for a moment.

Maybe Julie was right. Maybe they should put her father in a nursing home, then Sarah would be free to follow her heart. But at what price? She couldn't possibly build her happiness on her dad's misery, and she had no doubt that he'd be miserable away from his home, his family.

She pushed away from Jim and scrunched herself into the corner of the sofa.

"There's nothing you can do. I have to do this myself, Jim."

"Don't shut me out, Sarah. I realize you have responsibilities. I can help with your father. I *want* to help."

A tiny seed of hope began to germinate, but she quickly squashed it. What kind of life would that be for Jim, confined to the house, playing watchdog for a man he barely knew?

"No, Jim. I can't do that to you."

"What are you saying, Sarah?"

"Don't you see?" Her heart broke and she pressed her hands over the gaping wound. "I can't marry you."

Abruptly he got up and walked to the window, his back stiff. She'd wounded him. If not his heart, certainly his pride.

All of a sudden Sarah realized that he had never said he loved her. Did he? Was love implicit in a proposal? She wished she knew.

Staring at Jim's unyielding back she remembered all the ways he was wonderful. She couldn't sit on the sofa without making him understand.

Soundlessly she crossed the thick carpet, then put her hand softly on his arm.

"Jim?"

The wounded look on his face brought tears to her eyes.

"Please, *please* understand."

His eyes sought hers, and for a moment she thought everything was going to be all right. For a moment she thought he was going to smile at her in perfect understanding, then tell her that he would remain her friend. Always.

"You've been a wonderful friend to me."

"Is that all I've been for you, Sarah?"

*No!* She wanted to scream her denial. She wanted to fall into his arms and pour out her love for him.

Then what? Nothing had changed. She still couldn't marry him no matter how many declarations of love she made. The kindest thing she could do for the man she loved would be to let him go.

He mistook her silence for assent. With his face a cold mask, he walked out the door.

"I love you," Sarah cried. "I love you, Jim Standing Bear."

But there was no one to hear. The Bear had already gone. Out of her house. Out of her life.

Sarah woke in the middle of the night and found her father trying to climb over the garden wall. She finally got him inside, then fired the night sitter on the spot. Her third since Mrs. Grimes.

She cried that night, sitting in a chair beside her father's bed after he'd gone back to sleep. But she wasn't crying for him this time. She was crying for Jim, and for all she'd lost.

Jim woke in the middle of the night and decided to buy an airstrip. Why not? Flying was the only thing he had left, and thank God he had that. Otherwise he might go crazy. Could losing a woman drive a man crazy?

Summer was almost over before Sarah found the letter.

Sleep eluded her these days. She'd gone to her garden, not to dance but to mourn. Bone-weary and heartbroken, she sat beneath the outstretched wings of her broken angel.

She lifted her eyes to the rooftop next door. Jim wasn't there, of course. She'd known he wouldn't be. She hadn't seen him since the night he proposed.

So long ago. So very long ago.

Sarah sighed. At least she had that. He'd asked her to marry him. When she got back to the house she was going to turn back the pages of her desk calendar and mark the date, then put the calendar in the trunk with her other memorabilia.

A full moon lit her garden, and flowers perfumed the air. The flowers Jim had planted. Following the winding brick pathway, Sarah knelt to sniff and admire each precious blossom.

Memories overwhelmed her, and all of a sudden Sarah was so mad she shook her fists at the heavens.

"Why?" she whispered. "Why?"

She was still looking skyward when she saw a glimpse of gold in the angel's outstretched hand. Dragging a chair toward the statue, she climbed up and retrieved the music box her father had given her when she was six years old. He'd given Julie an identical one in silver.

The music began to play as soon as she lifted the lid, and inside lay her father's letter. She opened it up and began to read:

Sarah, this letter is for you because I know you'll be the one to try and sacrifice yourself for me. Both my daughters love me, of that I have no doubt. But Julie has always been the practical one. You're a caretaker, Sarah, and for that reason I worry what will happen to you when my mind is completely gone.

That's why I'm writing this letter. You'll try to take care of me yourself. Don't. I beg of you. I'm writing it down because you're at school and I can't tell you, and I don't know when, or if I'll have the mind to do this again.

The words blurred, and Sarah looked up at the moon and blinked back her tears. Then she read on:

Sweetheart, the thing you should know about this disease is that I'm happy in the world my failing mind has created. Time means nothing to me. Whether I see you and Julie every day or only once in a blue moon, it's all one and the same. I suppose this alternate reality is God's way of compensating for the dreadful loss.

Sarah glimpsed the brilliant mind she'd taken for granted. All her life she'd had access to a fount of wisdom and knowledge, and she hadn't fully appreciated it until she'd lost it.

I want you and Julie to find a reputable place for me staffed with compassionate nurses. It wouldn't hurt if they're pretty, either.

The old Dr. Sloan was shining through, and Sarah smiled through her tears.

This is the last thing I'll ever ask you to do, Sarah. Don't be noble and sacrifice yourself. Put me in a home! I mean that. No matter what happens remember, Sarah...tell Julie, too...I'll be loving you, always.

The tinkly sound of the music echoed his last refrain. Sarah closed her eyes and hummed along with the song. "Always."

"Let's take a little stroll through the clouds. What do you say?" Jim glanced at his brother sitting in the copilot's seat of the Baron.

"Go for it, pal. You know your way around the sky. Wish I could say the same thing for you on the ground."

"Let it drop, Ben."

The plane vanished into a thick cloud that looked like dirty banks of snow piled around them. Surrounded by the foglike thickness, Ben fell silent and Jim breathed a sigh of relief.

Sometimes he wished he'd never told his brother about his ill-fated proposal to Sarah. It still hurt just thinking her name, and Jim tried to push her out of his mind.

This time it didn't work. At fourteen thousand feet the plane shot out of the cloud into stunning brilliance.

"Wow!" Ben said.

"Ever seen the moon like this?"

"No. Man, oh, man." He looked at his brother. "I bet Sarah'd say *yes* if you'd bring her up here. It would be the perfect setting to tell her you love her.''

Jim hoped the expression on his face gave new meaning to the word *grim*. For once in his life, he wanted his baby brother to shut up.

But Ben had never been the kind to back away from a fray let alone a formidable expression.

''You *did* tell her you loved her, didn't you?'' Jim's silence damned him. ''Man, oh, man. Didn't I teach you anything about women?''

Grim vanished and morose took its place.

''I guess not.''

''Then it's about damned time I started.''


Julie and Sarah cried over the letter together, then they left Savannah in charge and set out to find a place for their father.

''It must have a place for dancing,'' Sarah said, and an all-day search turned up the perfect facility set in a lush garden.

They made hot tea, then pulled off their shoes and collapsed in Sarah's library.

''You know what this means, don't you, Sarah?''

Sarah didn't want to think about it. She had a Ph.D. in the school of disappointment.

''It means you're free. You can go to Jim and tell him how you feel. You can…''

''Don't.'' Sarah held up her hand to stop her sister's flow of words. ''I haven't seen him in months. What makes you think he'd even see me, let alone ask me to marry him?''

''What makes you think he wouldn't? Especially after what he's done for your boys.''

''What are you talking about?'

"You mean you don't know?"

"Know what?"

Julie rolled her eyes. "It's been in all the papers."

"I haven't had time to sit down in weeks, let alone read a paper." Delta would have told her if she hadn't been on leave for the birth of her first grandbaby. "Are you going to tell me or what?"

"Lieutenant Commander Jim Standing Bear bought a private airstrip, and he's teaching your boys to fly in his off-duty hours. He said that flying not only gives the boys a summer activity, but it also builds their self-esteem."

Julie gave her sister a triumphant smile. "He's a damned hero, Sarah. Again."

Love was a tornado ripping through her, tearing away pain and loneliness and fear.

Jim was rescuing *her* boys. He was doing it for *her.*

Or was he?

If he'd done it for her, why hadn't he come over to tell her so? And why had he never said, "Sarah, I love you"?

"Go to see him, Sarah."

What if he told her no? Sarah didn't think she could bear that.

"I can't, Julie. I just can't."

Julie didn't press the issue. Mainly, Sarah guessed, because they were too busy. Within a heartbreaking few days they had settled their father into Angelwood Manor.

Though they didn't need sitters, Savannah would still come every day so their father would have a familiar face, and a dance partner. His room was only two doors away from the recreation area, an enormous space with a player piano and a parquet floor.

When Sarah went home the empty house enveloped her. She had far too much space. And she was entirely too close to Jim. Tomorrow she was going to look for a smaller house, as far away from his neighborhood as she could get.

"What are you doing?" Julie asked when she called the next morning.

"House-hunting," Sarah said, then told her why.

"You'll do no such thing. Today we're going to the beach."

"Are you going to try to boss me around the rest of the summer?"

"No, only today." Julie giggled. "Put on something stunning."

"For the beach?"

"Well, yeah. You never know."

Sarah got suspicious when Julie headed toward the same stretch of isolated beach Jim had carried her to so long ago. Had it been months? Suddenly it seemed like yesterday.

"Close your eyes, Sarah," she said.

"Why?"

"Because I don't want to spoil the surprise."

"You have a surprise for me? That's sweet, Julie."

"Yeah, well, that's me. Sweet all the way to my dyed roots." She parked the car, cut the engine, then yelled, "Ta-dah!"

Sarah opened her eyes. There in the bay was a riverboat, and on the beach beside it was Jim Standing Bear. She turned to her sister in amazement.

"Julie...What in the world...?"

"Go to him." Julie gave her a gentle push. "Go and ask Jim."

Her heart beating like war drums, Sarah got out of the car and started toward Jim. The stretch of beach between them seemed endless.

There was no sound except the car engine as Julie pulled back onto the highway and headed home.

Now she was completely alone. Except for Jim.

She was glad she'd worn a dress, pink, a soft summery confection Julie had pulled out of her closet when she saw Sarah's gray sweatpants and white T-shirt.

"Good Lord, you look like an orphan," she'd said. "Here. Wear this."

Jim was still as a statue, watching her in agonizing silence. The wind whipped Sarah's skirt and the sand dragged at her feet. Then suddenly Jim was running, running toward her with his arms wide open.

Laughing, crying, she raced into his arms. He caught her up and held her so her feet were dangling and her face was two inches from his.

"I thought this day would never come," he said.

"Neither did I."

He began kissing her, and she slid down the length of his body until her feet were touching sand. But she was still floating. She might never stop.

Jim pulled back and cupped her face. "Let me look at you." His eyes, intense and shining, swept over her face until she was so flushed she thought she'd faint. "My God," he breathed. "How have I stayed away so long?"

He kissed her again, and she couldn't have said the exact moment he lifted her into his arms and carried her up the gangplank and into the riverboat. He didn't stop kissing her until they were inside an enormous ballroom with piped-in music and gleaming floors and silver balls spinning on the ceiling. Spinning as fast as Sarah's mind.

"This is for you, Sarah." He leaned over and left a trail of kisses from her mouth to her throat, then beyond, and it was only then that she realized they were all alone on the riverboat.

It was only then that she realized Jim had given her another of her dreams.

"Oh, Jim," she said, then words failed her. They probably always would in the presence of this magnificent man.

"I love you, Sarah. I've been loving you for so long I can't remember when it all started."

"I do," she whispered. "I loved you even before I met you. When I looked up and saw you on your rooftop watching over me in my garden, I loved you."

The lost words suddenly came tumbling out, and Sarah knew exactly what to say. Standing on tiptoe she pressed her lips softly against his, then leaned back, smiling.

"You are my hero, Jim. You'll always be my hero, and the answer to your question is *yes*. Yes, I'll marry you."

Laughing, he swung her into the air and spun her around until they were both dizzy and out of breath.

"If I'd stuck around longer when I first asked that question, is that the answer I'd have heard?"

"Maybe. Think of all the time we've lost."

She was feeling coy and mischievous and loving every minute of it. For a moment he looked genuinely crestfallen, then his recovery swept her off her feet. Literally.

Jim scooped her up and headed belowdecks. He didn't stop until he was in a large stateroom with a canopied bed.

"Just think of all the fun we're going to have making up for it, future Mrs. Standing Bear."

He spread her upon the bed as tenderly as if she were a bruisable flower. Then he lay down beside her and kissed her.

"Tell me," she said when they finally came up for air.

"Better yet. Why don't I show you?" he said.

And he did.

It was dark when they finally made it back to the ballroom.

"Dance for me, Sarah," he said.

And in bare feet and the white shirt Jim had worn, with the moon and stars sending showers of silver crystals over the shining floor, Sarah spread her arms and danced for the man she loved.

## *Epilogue*

Little Miss Elizabeth Standing Bear was an irrepressible three-year-old with her aunt Julie's flaming red hair and her daddy's dancing black eyes. As they crossed the flower-decked pathway that led to the entrance of Angelwood Manor, she tugged at her father's hand.

"Hur'we, Daddy. I want to see Poppa."

Laughing at his daughter's impatience, Jim scooped her up and carried her through the doorway on his shoulders, bending down so she wouldn't bang her head on the door frame.

Sarah smiled indulgently. She did a lot of that these days. That was because she had a lot to smile about. An adored and adoring husband, a beautiful daughter, and the precious son who lay in her arms blowing spit bubbles.

She caught up with them inside the door.

"Hello again, beautiful." Jim wrapped his free arm around her and kept it there when they entered her father's room.

His face lit up when he saw Elizabeth.

"Come here, little fairy princess," he said, holding out his arms.

Elizabeth never walked anywhere. She bounced and twirled and leaped. Savannah, who was sitting in a chair by the window, laughed and shook her head.

"Lordy, that child." She nodded toward Dr. Sloan. "If he don't set store by her, I don't know who does."

"Will 'ou dance wif me, Poppa?" Elizabeth climbed into her grandfather's lap and planted a big kiss on his cheek.

"Of course I will. Just let me get my top hat." He grinned at his visitors. "This little fairy princess comes to see me all the time. Calls me Poppa. I'm teaching her the soft shoe. Gene Kelly's jealous."

He paused to gaze at the baby in Sarah's arms. "And who's this?"

"This is Sloan Standing Bear," she told him as she did every week.

Her father leaned close and the baby latched on to his finger.

"I think he likes me."

"I'm certain he does," Sarah said softly, then they all went into the recreation room and her father went to the player piano to select a song.

Sarah held her breath, waiting to see what he would choose, and when the familiar melody filled the air, she smiled. She liked to believe that somewhere in his mind was a piece of memory that could never be lost. She liked to believe that week after week he chose the same song because he remembered, and, remembering, loved.

Her father took Elizabeth's tiny hands in his and began a stately waltz. Smiling, Jim walked toward Sarah and she passed the baby to Savannah.

Then she moved into her husband's arms and began to dance to the haunting strains of "Always."

\* \* \* \* \*

Beloved author
# Sherryl Woods

*is back with a brand-new miniseries*

# The Calamity Janes

## Five women. Five Dreams.
## A lifetime of friendship....

 On Sale May 2001—DO YOU TAKE THIS REBEL?
Silhouette Special Edition

On Sale August 2001—COURTING THE ENEMY
Silhouette Special Edition

On Sale September 2001—TO CATCH A THIEF
Silhouette Special Edition

 On Sale October 2001—THE CALAMITY JANES
Silhouette Single Title

On Sale November 2001—WRANGLING THE REDHEAD
Silhouette Special Edition

"Sherryl Woods is an author who writes with a very
special warmth, wit, charm and intelligence."
—*New York Times* bestselling author
Heather Graham Pozzessere

*Available at your favorite retail outlet.*

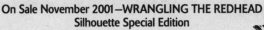 *Silhouette*®
Where love comes alive™

Silhouette Books and
award-winning, bestselling author

# LINDSAY McKENNA

are proud to present

# MORGAN'S MERCENARIES:
## IN THE BEGINNING...

These first stories

## HEART OF THE WOLF
## THE ROGUE
## COMMANDO

introduce Morgan Trayhern's *Perseus Team*—
brave men and bold women who travel
the world righting wrongs, saving lives...
and resisting love to their utmost.
They get the mission done—but rarely escape
with their hearts intact!

*Don't miss these exciting stories available in April 2001—
wherever Silhouette titles are sold.*

Silhouette®
*Where love comes alive*™

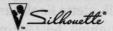